The Copper Tale

Stephen S. Stallings

PROLOGUE

Year 913

The architecure of the Mississippi watershed is as old as that of Egypt. Though composed of other materials than the sandstone of the pyramids, the monuments of the Mississippi are as large in size and as regular in shape. Indeed, one of the most noteworthy qualities of ancient American architecture is that some of its forms were so regular that they were replicated precisely in locations many miles apart.

-Roger G. Kennedy

Hidden Cities

Huarangial took a deep drag on his pipe and watched the sun take her time going down behind the city of Xanach. His house sat perched on a small ridge running along the eastern edge of the city's sprawling complex of homes, shops, roads and temples just a half-day's walk south of the confluence where the Missouri joins the Mississippi. He loved to sit on his small porch and watch the city bustle toward evening with the great central pyramid framed in the reddening light of the setting sun. He was old now, but much of his life had been spent bustling along with the rest: trading and dealing; buying and selling; earning friends and placating enemies. Now he was enjoying the fruits of a lifetime of effort. His life had settled into a comfortable, if unexciting, routine of watching sports and smoking the best of his aged smokeweed. Huarangial's biggest complaints were that it had become hard to find a good ball game to watch or a lively friend to smoke with. The northern style of ball game he'd grown up playing was passing out of style in favor of the southern game of *pitz*, a game of hip bounces and heavy rubber balls Huarangial thought ridiculous.

His wife of thirty six years had passed more than a decade ago and his once large circle of friends had dwindled into a small group of cantankerous old coots too decrepit to stay up late gambling and telling jokes as they used to do. Dwinchel, though, remained stout, stopping by most afternoons to talk of politics or sports or the glorious past, and today he sat on an old stump next to Huarangial pulling tobacco smoke from an ancient stone pipe of his own. He had a habit, sometimes unpleasant, sometimes amusing, of laughing without cause.

"Gial," he said after an unprompted guffaw, "do you remember that night we lost the ball game to the White River Clan? When that big lug Buchee cheated?"

Huarangial grunted, took another puff, and said, "they might of beat us anyway, but he did trip me, the dog."

Dwinchel laughed again, leading to a nasty coughing fit. After a deep breath and another drag he said, "there was something else Buchee did that game that I was thinking of. Do you remember the penalty?"

Huarangial thought it through. "Was he put in the box for fighting?"

Dwinchel laughed again. "No Gial. Your memory stinks. He was tossed for stopping! He just stood still in the middle of the game staring at you while everyone swirled around him. The referee nearly threw him out of the game."

Huarangial paused and took another puff. He looked out over Xanach, enjoying the dusky scene of activity around the great pyramid. The smell of tens of thousands of cooking fires filled his nostrils. He wondered how anyone could live out in the country, far from the vibrancy of city life. "It was because of what I called him," he said, "but I can't remember what I said."

Dwinchel looked at him crosswise. "You are losing your memory, old man." he said. "You called him a 'giant-spawn'! Stopped him dead in his tracks. He didn't know whether to laugh or punch you. The referee called the penalty while he stood there trying to decide."

Huaranshee smiled. He now remembered hurling the insult, a slur so ancient few even remembered why it was insulting. He took a puff of the smokeweed deep into his old lungs and sat back, smiling as he let the smoke flow from his lips and rise through the cool late summer air in lazy waves and circles. He stretched his long legs before him, savoring the irony. He knew now what he did not know then. It was he, Huarangial, who was a spawn of giants. And it did not bother him at all.

Part I

The Land

Spring, Year 472

[T]he Western Hemisphere before 1492. . .was, in the current view, a thriving, stunningly diverse place, a tumult of languages, trade, and culture, a region where tens of millions of people loved and hated and worshipped as people do everywhere. Much of this world vanished after Columbus. . .

-Charles C. Mann

1491

ONE

TIANATI'S LAST BATTLE

The sun rose behind the hill held by the People's soldiers, lighting last night's dewy battlefield with a ruse of peaceful light. Tianati peered south up the ridgeline to a rocky pine-topped outcrop a few hundred feet distant. Something rustled in the chokeberry thicket beneath the pines. He wondered if the sentries were finally checking in. They were already late.

Tianati breathed in the air. He could smell early spring flowers, a hint of coming rain, and blood from yesterday's clash. From far away, he thought he could catch a hint of the first burnings of the year. Even in the midst of the long war the People lit the fires on schedule. There was no smell of black atsik, however. The company's lazy cook still slept. *Just as well*, thought Tianati, *he can't brew atsik for scat*. Even without his morning drink, Tianati had been awake for hours. His fitful sleep had started with dreams of the dying, like every night, but just before he woke songs from ancient parties floated through his head, as if peace was in the offing for the first time in a decade. *No chance of that*, he thought.

The previous morning the soldiers had gathered to plan for the day's battle, with some hoping they would drive the giant Allegh warriors away in defeat, that the rebellion that threatened to upend the

People's well-ordered world would finally be crushed. Tianati had cautioned otherwise, having seen the dark resolve glinting from several black Allegh eyes during the previous day's bloody clash. He had come of age just over ten years ago, and the People had been at war with the Allegh rebels for his entire adult life. The war had begun while Tianati was still away on his post-Naming mission, and he had joined the fight as soon as he returned.

Nearly a decade of fighting the giant rebels had made Tianati into a seasoned and effective warrior, even if he showed less relish for blood than others, and his opinion carried some weight with the other, mostly younger, soldiers. His pessimism the day before had been warranted. A heavy rain had slowed the People's troops and made their atlatls and bows less effective. The giants had driven them back with a relentless push from the left, hemming the soldiers in atop the narrow fortified ridge that had been their base for much of the winter.

As dawn unfolded into morning, ozonated winds cooled the air, threatening more spring storms. The soldiers along Tianati's line prepared their weapons and chose their positions on the edge of the hill, waiting and watching for giants. Tianati searched the outcrop for signs that the sentries were awake. He thought he caught a movement, but in an instant a thousand gray birds lifted as one from the thicket in a screeching, twisting mass, briefly blocking the rising sun. He turned his head and followed their flight up and over the oaks behind the soldier's main camp. It was a mistake. A heavy spear hit the ground less than a body length from his left foot with a dull *thunk*.

"Giants!" he hollered towards the main camp. "Giants attacking!" The charge came from a clump of leafless oak trunks on the ridge just below the piney outcrop. And it came fast. The giant Allegh warriors could cover lots of ground in very little time. Their well-muscled seven-foot frames were suited to the uneven terrain. The hilltop where the People's soldiers had made their camp was somewhat protected by steep slopes on three sides, with low earthen walls running along the edges. But to the south, a narrow ridge dipped only slightly from the wall before rising again to join a high, rocky outcrop topped with tall pines. The outcrop's rocky slopes seemed too steep for even giants to negotiate without great difficulty, but the soldiers had left three sentries atop it to guard against climbing giants anyway; giants often surprised with their feats of physicality. Now, in the brightening morning light, Tianati could see the bodies of slaughtered sentries sprawled on the high slopes, and at least a hundred giants charging toward the People's camp. *They must have climbed the cliffs in the night,* he thought. *Why do we always underestimate the cleverness of these giants?*

Tianati still felt confident. Three hundred and sixty well-armed, well-fed soldiers of the People held a strong defensive position behind the low berms perched on the hilltop. The People's soldiers repulsed the initial charge, but the giants regrouped and began advancing slowly to find weak points in the line, using scattered oaks as haphazard shields.

It began to rain again about an hour after the first charge, with steady, large drops. The water made both weapons and footing unreliable, and slowed the pace of the battle to a horrible slog. Scores fell, but neither the Allegh nor the People seemed to gain an advantage. The battle lasted all day, and fell into an oddly rhythmic pattern, with the Allegh thrusting forward in groups of three or four with their large, heavy spears, looking for a spot to break through, and the People's soldiers countering by pouring atlatl darts and arrows into the giants' ranks from behind the berms.

As the sun slipped down behind Tianati's left shoulder, the giants began massing at the point of the line just opposite him, sensing the terrain and thin concentration of soldiers at that point favored an Allegh charge. Tianati knew that he and the thirty soldiers on this berm would have to hold the line themselves or fall back. To his left, another fifty men held a larger berm that protected Tianati's flank and could serve as a fall-back position. To his right and directly behind him was the steep edge of the hill.

"Tianati! Fall back! You can't hold that line!" his friend Garank called out through the light rain, lowering his bow and pulling an arrow from a pouch on his back. Garank was among a small group of soldiers using the new bows to launch arrows. They claimed to be able to hit targets with more reliability than atlatl users. Tianati disagreed. He thought the bowmen were usually just poor atlatl throwers, and that the darts launched by the thin gut-strings of the bows packed less of a punch than those whipped forward by a well-tuned atlatl in a strong arm. But he was old-fashioned when it came to war.

Tianati shook his head and shouted back. "No — I can hold them here." He tried to sound confident, but he doubted that his unit could actually hold the small berm for long if the Allegh charged with more than thirty of their giant warriors. He was also running out of darts.

He loaded one of his last three darts into his atlatl, tuned the pitch of the weighted rocks notched halfway up the shaft, and waited. The setting sun's lower lip pouted under the heavy clouds, barely throwing off enough light to illuminate the early spring underbrush on the thin ridgeline. *Three darts, fading light, and angry giants*, Tianati thought wryly, *not turning into such a great evening after all.*

The rain falling through the sunlight turned as bright as ice, catching Tianati's eye. He let himself look at it a second too long. The point of a spear flew within a hand's breadth of his right ear. "Dammit," he swore out loud at himself, "got to focus!" The giant who threw the spear ran in great leaping strides across the muddy sward towards Tianati's post. Tianati took aim and scored a hit on the giant's shoulder, and the Allegh fell. But he was just the vanguard of the new charge. At least forty more came out from behind the oaks with a loud, low yell like only giants could make.

Tianati scored hits with each of his last two darts. He looked around and found that half his fellow soldiers had fallen back to Garank's line. The remainder took hurried shots, leaving thirty healthy giants armed with twelve-foot spears running full speed at Tianati's position. Behind and to Tianati's left, Garank drew back his fancy new bow. *That will never stop them*, Tianati thought, and pulled his heavy club from his belt. The handle was wet from the rain, but Tianati had no choice; he was out of atlatl darts. Garank managed to shoot a small arrow into a giant's thigh, but it seemed to have little effect on the large man's charge. *Piece of scat arrows*, thought Tianati. The giant continued to hurl himself with great bounds towards the slope.

When the giant reached the bottom of Tianati's berm, just three strides away from the top, he looked down for just a moment to gain sound footing on the wet hillside. Tianati did not hesitate. He jumped as soon as the giant looked down. The last thing the giant saw was his own oversized foot plunging into the mud as Tianati's war club crushed his heavy skull. Tianati grabbed the long spear from the Allegh's dying hand and ran back up the hill to re-take his position. He couldn't hurl the spear, at least not with enough force to do damage—it was too heavy. Instead, he drove its butt end into the ground and kept it pointing at the giants to discourage a direct charge.

"Duck!" Garank yelled. Tianati obeyed – just in time. A friendly volley of small arrows flew over his head, driving back half the charging giants just as they were preparing to launch spears at Tianati's line. *Maybe those arrows aren't so bad after all*, he mused.

With the giants reeling from the arrows, the time was right to turn them back. Tianati rallied his remaining soldiers for a charge down the hill. Twenty soldiers followed him with war clubs raised, yelling a People's war chant in fearsome unison. Tianati lost track of his comrades as he whirled and spun amongst the giants, cracking knees, punching stomachs, and dodging fists and spear points. When he could see no more giants and could barely lift his club, Garank clapped him on the shoulder and leaned into him with a big smile. "Come on back, Tianati. The Allegh have retreated for the night."

Tianati scanned the battlefield, taking a moment to ensure the giants were truly driven back and to count the dead. Only then did he stagger back to the berm and take a position next to Garank. Looking down the ridge in the dying light he thought he could still count the shapes of fifty or more giants shuffling behind their nighttime line, waiting for a chance to avenge their fallen comrades in the morning. *This battle is a long way from over,* Tianati thought.

TWO

THE ALLEGH'S GAMBIT

The rain felt good on Berengial's head. He knew that the rain was also good news for the Allegh troops. The swift warriors of the Littles would be slowed in the mud, and their weapons of hurl and twang would become wet and inaccurate. Anything that forced the Littles into close hand-to-hand combat helped the Allegh. Any one Little would be no match for Berengial or any of his fellow Allegh warriors. Berengial was over seven feet tall and weighed nearly three hundred pounds. His comrades were of similar stature, while each Little grew to only about five and three-quarters feet high, and weighed half of what an Allegh weighed. But the Littles were far more numerous and quite skilled with their atlatls and bows. Like deadly mosquitos.

Berengial was on the right side of the thin Allegh battle line. *So many dead*, he thought. The line was about a third of the strength he would have wanted for a battle like this. *We have to end this war before we are all gone.* As he checked his spear point, he realized the Allegh would have to do something different if they were to end the decade-long war that had taken the best of his people, and gained the Allegh next to nothing. *They still fear us*, he thought. *They call us "monsters," "giants," and they probably hate this war even more than we do. If we can use their fear and their hope for peace in just the right way . . .*

He would raise the matter tonight at the captains' meeting. *Whatever we decide, we have to give ourselves some breathing room right now*, he thought. He tightened his grip on his spear, looked to his cousin on the right and his friend on the left, and let out at a deep, strong yell as only the Allegh people could. After a ferocious charge and a few hours of close, bloody work, the Littles were pushed back into their small hilltop earthen fort, thinking they'd won the day.

That night, the Allegh captains gathered around a fire well behind the lines. The first business was to name and honor those who'd died in the day's battle. The captains then discussed the plans for tomorrow. After the pressing business had been handled and the next day's orders given to the warriors, Didigial, the current Allegh leader, opened the floor to the captains to raise any new matters. Berengial spoke first. "We may or may not win this battle, but there are ten Little armies of similar size within a few days' march. Every month we lose more warriors. Our villages are emptying. We have to strike a peace deal."

Didigial frowned. He had been chosen by a random throw of the gambling sticks to serve as leader for a year, as was the Allegh custom. Berengial thought luck had betrayed the Allegh with his selection. He was too big on talk for Berengial's taste, and his vigor in battle never matched his rhetoric. "If we go to the Littles to plead for peace, they will think we are weak and strike even harder," Didigial said. Several captains nodded in agreement. Berengial began to despair that reason would prevail.

Pollangial stood to speak. He was the not the largest or strongest of the captains, but his instincts in matters of war planning were sound. "Perhaps there is a third way," he said quietly. The other Allegh captains listened carefully. "We could make an overture for peace, make it convincing, and when the Littles are finally lured into complacency, when their armies have all gone back to deer hunting, when their cities and towns turn to dancing instead of marching, when their craftsmen make pipes instead of arrows and darts, when they have gone back to sleep," he paused and looked around into each of the gathered captains' eyes, "then, we destroy them—completely and totally destroy them."

The group sat quiet for some time as they thought about Pollangial's plan. "It won't work," said Berengial finally. "We can never kill enough of them. They will come back to take revenge one day. This won't end the war, just prolong it."

"I think we should do what Pollangial suggests," Didigial said. He turned to Berengial. "I respect you, Berengial, but you offer no good alternative. Tomorrow, we'll approach the Littles' captains and start to talk 'peace.'"

Berengial resigned himself to losing the argument on the overall strategy, but he thought their tactical approach could be better; while he would have chosen a different gambit, if this was to be the Allegh's plan, he wanted it to have the best chance of success. "Wait," said Berengial, "if this is the path we will take, let's be smart about it. Don't approach them here, at the scene of an equal battle. Let's take some stout Allegh warriors and strike into the heart of their realm, the big earthen circles and octagons where they hold their ceremonies and gaze at the moon. They expect no attack there, and only priests will await us. If we don't kill them, they will quiver with gratitude and trust us all the more." He turned and spat. "If we're going to try to destroy them, let's at least do it right."

Pollangial nodded at Berengial with respect. The rest of the Allegh captains murmured their approval. "Then it is done," said Didigial. "I will send messengers to the rest of the Allegh troops with instructions on how to act once the 'peace' is reached." He turned back to Berengial. "As a reward for your idea, you will lead the group into the Little's heartland. You should leave before dawn. Take no more than ten warriors. We will need as much strength as possible here to keep this battle at a draw while you are gone."

Berengial left the captains' meeting in a foul mood, but he was a loyal captain. He gathered ten of the best Allegh warriors to accompany him and they jogged out of camp hours before the dawn.

They marched for a day and a night without resting. On the second day, they built a raft for two days of river travel, and then hiked overland for another two days, pausing to sleep for a solid day before resuming the march. They ate only dried meat and nuts. On the sixth day they saw the valley where the Littles had their big festivals. They mustered all the stealth they possessed to sneak into the heart of the Littles' ceremonial center, but they needn't have worried; no warriors guarded the place. The Littles never suspected such a bold incursion. The squad of battle-hardened Allegh warriors met only a handful of the Littles' priests and without a fight they now occupied the great circle at the heart of the Littles' sacred world. Berengial ushered the priests together on the falcon-shaped mound at the circle's center. "Which one of you is in charge here?"

An old man, slightly shorter and thinner than the rest, stepped forward. "I am the Chief Astronomer. If you must spill blood, kill me and leave the others. They are not warriors, merely star gazers."

Berengial laughed. "We are not here to kill you. I come to offer peace."

The Chief Astronomer raised his eyebrows, and peered up into Berengial's still smiling face. "Peace?" He laughed, but with derision, not humor. "Such a thing no longer seems possible."

Berengial's smile faded. "Little, do you think I sprinted across a hundred miles and risked my neck on the river to debate with you? I come with a real offer. So long as you can guarantee us our lands, all lands surrounding the waters that flow into the river that bears our people's name, and authority over these lands, and put it in one of your fancy bead strings, I will guarantee the end of hostilities, fighting any Allegh who violates the agreement myself."

Berengial had chosen his demands carefully. He had calculated that a truce offer that left the People's world intact but contained enough concessions to satisfy the more belligerent Allegh would appear to the Littles to be a real offer, an offer that would not unduly arouse suspicion.

The priests looked uncomfortable and stayed quiet, still expecting to be killed, while Berengial finished his demands. The Chief Astronomer, however, stepped closer to stand toe to toe with Berengial. He looked up into his deep still eyes, as if searching for a lost gem. Finally he spoke.

"I will seek approval of such a deal from the People's Council. Will you join me for a meal so we can talk about the details? Then I will have one of our priests craft the bead string and send runners to the People's City."

"We are always happy to eat Little food. Tell your runners to be swift. This war must end now."

THREE

STRANGE SONGS

For weeks after the surprise attack on the hillside fortifications where Tianati was stationed, the People and the giants stared at each other across the battlefield. Some days they skirmished and fought to a standstill. Most days they stayed huddled in their camps, the commanders citing weather or injuries as reasons for taking a hiatus from the fighting.

On this day there was no fighting, as a ferocious spring storm raged overhead. Neither side seemed keen on a battle. Now night began to creep onto the hill where the People still held their position. The People's soldiers built a fire to the side of their defensive position, so that the light was cast out onto the contested sward. The captains posted soldiers in evenly-spaced pickets to warn of any overnight approaches by the enemy.

Tianati's picket was far to the right and in front of the main camp, as removed from the fire as any of the pickets. There was a full moon, but the clouds were thick and it was dark. He could see less than fifteen feet through the moist night air. After three hours of guard duty, Tianati took his turn at trying to sleep, but he had to force his eyes closed. Then, at the edge of his hearing, there were strains of distant songs. Sure it was just another strange dream, he kept his eyes closed. But the singing persisted, and grew louder, and was familiar. Tianati opened his eyes.

Oh the lines know

And the road goes on

Straight and long

Heed this song

The fickle Moon she glows

and the mighty Sun he shows

the way to grow

the way to know

the way to keep the People strong

The slow cadence picked up with the quick-beated chorus known to all the People:

Oh the square and octagon

Moon and Sun and circle high

We mark the time 'til Kysus night

and we welcome restless strangers

Oh the square and octagon

Moon and Sun and circle low

We mark the time 'til war is done

and we seek our spirit brothers

Moon and Sun and flame aglow

Bear can see the way to go

Moon and Sun and pipe of weed

We can see the sacred mountain

It's still a ways away

It's still a ways away

If it were not for the need to keep his position hidden from the giants, Tianati would have chanted the last two lines along with the mysterious marchers. But he heard something else, even stranger, in the sound of the song. He heard voices of giants singing along. And not from the enemy Allegh position up the ridge—no, the singing came from far up the valley. Soon Tianati could see torches bobbing along beside the stream. A group of giants and People's soldiers was marching toward the camp. *Marching together*, thought Tianati.

The group of singers stopped a mile away from the hilltop battle-field and built a large bonfire. They began to control the ebb and flow of the fire to create a familiar rhythm of light and smoke and started a new song. The tune was an old one that Tianati knew well, but most of the words were unfamiliar:

The legend of earth comes from Raven on down

and tells of the first of the People

Tianati knew that line. But the words that followed were strange, new, and joyous:

> *The War, Raven said, is now just an old tale*
>
> *In the Burning Month of this Hawk Year*
>
> *The Giants and People are once again one*
>
> *The rivers and hills are at peace*
>
> *The large and the many, the rebels and People*
>
> *Have ended their long game of blood!*

A cheer erupted from the People's camp, and another deeper yell came from the Allegh camp on the hill. No one relinquished his position, however. War had been too bloody for too long to trust a few lines of a song from travelers in the night. But all the warriors hoped the morning would bring a message of real peace.

$$\text{☽ ● ☾}$$

In the morning a single messenger arrived in each of the warring camps bearing the same message. The People's messenger announced during breakfast that peace had indeed been reached. Tianati ate happily with Garank.

"What was peace like?" asked Garank. He had been only ten years old when the war started.

Tianati laughed. "More food, less death. More singing, less killing."

"How did it start? I mean, what really happened?"

Tianati looked at the young soldier. The official version was well known. The giants had been friends and allies of the People for centuries. When other nations had been foolish enough to wage war on the alliance, the numbers and resources of the People combined with the ferocious strength of the giants had been unbeatable. In return, the giants had enjoyed all the benefits of the People's empire in full bloom. They had joined in the People's games and celebrations, shared in the bountiful harvests, and lived in an unusual harmony with the People. War seemed unthinkable. Then a small group of giants hungry for power and glory incited a rebellion, convincing their brethren to join in a war of aggression against the People. At least, that was what the priests and the People's Council hoped that everyone would believe.

But Tianati knew it wasn't the truth. The trouble had really started with the fires. The People had always burned vast swaths of the land on certain pre-calculated dates; small local fires every year in the spring to clear underbrush, replenish the soils, and produce fertile forests and meadows; large regional conflagrations every few years to restore the overall health of the forests and plains. After centuries of managing the land with fire, the People had the methods and timings of the burns down to a precise science. Elaborate earthworks – huge mound observatories – were built near every major settlement to help the People track the motions of the heavens so the dates of the burns could be coordinated across vast distances. The People trained their brightest young boys and girls to become Astronomers who watched the skies and charted the movements of the stars, planets, sun, and moon over the course of nights, months, years, and centuries. The earthen observatories were built to precise geometric alignments to allow the Astronomers to track solstices, lunar maximums and minimums, planetary precessions, and other heavenly movements.

The Astronomers recorded their observations in calendars made of inscribed stone tablets, bead strings, and woven belts. They relied upon their calendars to tell the People when to plant, when to burn, when to celebrate, and when to mourn. They tried to coordinate the major regional burns to all occur on the same day so that the People would know to take shelter in the town centers and ceremonial earthworks, places carefully cleared and groomed so as to have no trees, brush or other flammable material. Fire signal towers graced the high prominences near most major towns. Fire and smoke signals leapt from tower to tower to confirm the times for burnings and major ceremonies. The fires were the People's gardening tool, and the result was a landscape fruitful, easy to traverse, and full of well-fed deer, bison, elk and fowl. The People had created a rich and sustaining land by wielding flames with precision and exceptionally good timing.

For centuries, the People had grown in numbers because of the bounty yielded by their fire-controlled agriculture. They had spread deeper into lands to the north and east around the Allegh's River, lands long home to the giants. The giants in these remote lands, however, were not well integrated into the People's culture, and were not informed of the burns beforehand. When more of the People began moving into remote Allegh haunts and spreading the area of their burns, many giants lost their homes, and some lost their lives. The indiscriminate fires turned many families of giants from friends to foes of the People, fueling discontent and distrust.

Eager to maintain good will with the giants, the People's Astronomers tried to warn giants living near their towns of upcoming burns so they could take shelter. But one made a fatal mistake. A junior Astronomer assigned to a frontier town two days march from the Allegh's River had built his observatory on poor alignments, and misjudged the passage of the moon. The town had yet to build a fire signal tower, and had to rely on the Astronomer's calendar to confirm the date for the fires. He ordered the fires started half a month too early. Young men from the town spread potent fuel through the forest at places designed to speed and intensify the burn. Nearby, several families of giants had gathered in a steep valley for a wedding party, thinking the fires were still half a month away. Over fifty giants, including many children, died as the well-fueled flames washed into the gorge from three sides. No amount of reparation or apology from the People was enough, and the giants took their revenge by slaughtering all the People in the town. The bungling Astronomer suffered a particularly gruesome fate; a giant warrior poured a remnant of the People's own fuel down his throat and lit a fuse in his mouth, burning him from within. War had spread with the speed of the fires after that. A large number of People, and even many giants, had fled the fighting and traveled a great distance to the ancient homeland of both the People and the Allegh far to the south in Zialand. Little was known of their fate, but their departure weighed heavily on the consciences of both sides during the war.

Tianati thought about this tragic bungle of a war as he looked at Garank. "Some stupid Astro started his fires too early, killing lots of giants. I suppose the giants didn't like us burning their children. Hard to blame them," he said.

☽ ● ☾

The terms of the truce were sent forth in multiple duplicate bead strings borne by messengers, the order and shape of the strung shells, copper, mica, and polished stones conveying a meaning as rich as any written language to a skilled reader. Tianati could read and write with the beads as well as anyone; his skills at creating bead strings capable of delivering detailed information about battles and enemy positions was such that he had become the company's reluctant scribe. Creating the delicate bead necklaces made him feel like an old grandmother, but no one else in the company had near the skill he had at putting together coherent strings. The lives of his comrades depended on getting accurate information to the chiefs about the battles, and conveying the correct orders to the troops. Now he was the one picked to read the string and convey the terms of the treaty to the other men. He read the string first to himself, silently, telling the men he wanted to get it right the first time. As he fingered the bead string, he realized that the peace had not come cheap for the People. The Allegh would be restored to full rights as members of the People, with access to the People's City; the observatories; the ceremonial octagons, circles, and squares; the hunting grounds; the flint quarries; the rivers, streams, and roads. They would be welcomed again to the Naming ceremony and the Kysus festival. In return, the Allegh would fight alongside the People again, instead of against them, and the People's elaborate and wonderful infrastructure would stay safe from the ravages of war.

But there was something else in the treaty, a point that was uncomfortable for Tianati personally. The river above Point Town and all lands leading down to it would belong to the Allegh and the Allegh alone. None of the People could hunt there, fish there, live there, or worship there without approval from the Allegh council. The selection of the local Astronomers in the Allegh's lands would be subject to veto by the Allegh. Fires lit out of time would result in death for the Astronomer. The giants would be the only members of the People with such special dispensations. Tianati did not like the peace deal for that reason. He felt it would plant the seed for dissension and the eventual unraveling of the People's world and more war. But there was another reason, much more personal. His hometown was right in the heart of the Allegh's new country, a frontier outpost nestled in a hidden, leafy valley watered by a quick little stream that ran into the Allegh's river about eleven miles up from Point Town. In the fifty years since its founding, the People had built a small but well-groomed observatory, a ceremonial square-circle complex, and a great house for the council and other meetings in the town. There were five hundred of the People living within an hour's walk of the center of town. Tianati's own modest house was three miles from the observatory, on the north side of a bowl-shaped hill, protected from the winter winds and watered by a spring that bubbled with fresh, clear water. His sister and cousins all lived nearby, and the ashes of his mother and father were entombed under the town's mound. He knew the ways of the local deer and bison, called at least two old bears by name, and could find the sweetest berries with his eyes closed. But now, after years of killing giants, he would have to beg them for the right to stay in his own home.

$$\text{☽ ● ☾}$$

The last battle of the war had been fought in a remote, sparsely populated hilly country several days' march from the great northerly bend of the Ohio River. Tianati and his fellow soldiers waited until the giants had cleared out before decamping as one jubilant group toward the south. A large group broke off toward the west the next day, and at every trailhead smaller and smaller contingents broke off to head towards their respective hometowns. At a three-way fork in the road, Tianati, Garank and four other soldiers broke with the larger remaining group and headed towards the northeast frontier of the People's lands. Their spirits were high, but they remained wary. They had no way of knowing whether they might encounter straggling groups of giants who had yet to hear of the peace. When Tianati's turn walking the lead point ended, he allowed his mind to wander over the past decade of war: the battles fought, the scores of friends and cousins lost. Despite his misgivings about the peace terms, he was glad to be going home. While his steps were light, his spirit was weary to its core.

FOUR

A SOLDIER'S WELCOME

The day Tianati returned to his hometown was dry and warm. His half-sister, Apeni, sat on the stoop of her aunt's house near the town center. She had a clear view down the road about a mile, and looked up from her beads every few minutes to see if he was coming, having heard the story of the war's end, like all of the People in town, from the fire tower keeper. Each fire tower was built on a hill or bluff chosen because it commanded a clear view of the other towers up and down the chain, and the signals leapt from tower to tower. A keeper lived in each tower, watching for signals to relay. A chain of fire towers stretched unbroken for over a thousand miles along the rivers from points north of Tianati's town to the People's City on the Ohio river far to the west and south, down further west to the confluence of the Ohio and the Mississippi, with tendrils connecting hundreds of towns and cities like a glistening spider-web straddling the world's most fertile drainage. The messages that could be sent by fire were limited to simple news and announcements. The message sent to the keeper in Tianati's town had been a short combination of colors, intensity, and smoke patterns that said simply: "War Ends! Peace!" The keeper had joyfully sent the same signal to his upstream colleague, confirmed receipt by watching his colleague re-transmit the signal, and then had run down the hill to the village to tell the Astronomer, who gathered whoever was nearby to announce the news. Apeni had been preparing turtle meat for stew when she heard the shouting, and a big grin broke out on her face as she thought of her older brother coming home. Just as quickly she scowled, suddenly worried that he had been hurt or killed just as the war was ending. *He could be the last to die*, she thought. She had spent the rest of the week vacillating between fear and joy, barely sleeping, passing the time with chores and bead stories like the one she read now.

The beads were made of worn copper and small shells from a distant coast. When handled by her practiced fingers, they told a story. Some of the bead combinations were standard: a pair of small cockle shells followed by a copper disk and three round beads, for example, was the traditional manner of introducing a humorous story involving animals. Different bead combinations indicated different animals. A string of seven small, round beads bracketed by tube shells was a snake, three irregular little copper disks a raven. Other combinations were not standard, serving more as unique mnemonic reminders of songs and stories for the individual reader.

Her grandmother had given her this bead story when she was very young, and had gone over it with her again and again to teach her its tale. Apeni returned to it when she wanted comfort. It was one of many stories about a hapless boy named Grenaga who always started off by making a big mistake. Only after the comedic intercession of some animal did he remedy his error. In this story, Grenaga tried to enslave all the birds to do his bidding, with poor results. A raven played a series of tricks on him to demonstrate how foolish the scheme was. Usually the story made Apeni laugh, but today it seemed different; somehow the characters seemed darker, the outcome less certain, the feeling more morose. She didn't know whether she understood the story better now that she was a woman, or whether her fear for Tianati clouded her reading of the beads. She turned a blue mussel shell over slowly, following the carefully-drawn lines and indents with her eyes and fingers, then a copper bead, then another two shells, then a few beads, hearing the characters in her head speak as she read the shape of this story's ending:

"Raven shall be given his freedom," called Grenaga, "and no one shall call him slave."

"Thank you Grenaga," said Raven. To show his thanks, Raven returned the seeds he had hidden in his wings. "I ask only one more thing: when you grow this sunflower, let me share in the crops grown by your people."

"We'll see," Grenaga laughed, "we will see my dark friend!!"

Apeni finally smiled. Grenaga was her favorite bead character. Her grandmother had given her many Grenaga bead stories. They always ended with a laugh. Her smile turned into a laugh of her own then, as she looked up to see Tianati, Garank, and twenty other soldiers running down the road. They stopped only long enough to pay respects at the town's altar. Apeni couldn't swear to it, but it seemed they cut short the ceremony and laughingly resumed their sprint into town.

"Api!" Tianati called, "Make us some groshi!" Garank and the other soldiers laughed. Groshi was a stiff fermented brew reserved for weddings, funerals, and other major ceremonies. A skilled brewer would need at least a month to prepare a single batch.

"I drank it all myself Tianati," Apeni called back, "it was the only way I could bear your return." The other soldiers howled at the insult; Tianati's little sister always gave as good as she got.

When Tianati was close enough that Apeni did not have to run to reach him, she took three dignified steps and hugged him deeply. She did not let her feelings show too much—that would be unseemly. Instead, she allowed herself only a quick, sincere smile. But she kept looking in Tianati's eyes, lowered her voice, and grew serious. "Tianati, the Astronomer left word that he wanted to see you as soon as you arrived. He said it was important." She let her smile return, but teasingly. "Bet you're in trouble."

"What can he do to me, send me to fight giants! Did he say what he wanted?"

"Nope. But hey, cheer up. I asked old Nokitis to make a bag for you. He gifted it too! Smell this." Apeni handed Tianati a small leather pouch filled with dried leaf, mixed as only Nokitis could mix. "There's one for you, too, Garank," she said, handing the soldier a bag of his own smokeweed.

Tianati put his face to the opening of the bag and breathed in the scent of the herbs, then exhaled slowly. "I missed old Nokitis' mixes, no doubt. What does he call this one?"

"Welcome Home Soldier." Apeni smiled warmly at Tianati and Garank. "He missed you too, I guess."

Apeni caught Garank looking at her with a little too much warmth, and saw Tianti give him a warning scowl. She laughed. "Maybe I'll mix up some groshi after all!" she said, winking at Garank to irritate her brother.

"Guess I better go see our friendly village Astronomer," Tianati said. "I'm sure he just wants to give me a fresh tobacco mix too. Come on Garank, escort me so I don't get exiled for saying something dumb."

$$\text{☽ ● ☾}$$

Tianati's town was nearly a half-month away by canoe from the People's City when traveling down-river, and more than a month by river, road and trail to return. The Great Observatory, site of the Naming ceremony and home to the Chief Astronomer, was at a similar distance. The Astronomer assigned to Tianati's village reflected its remote status. He was young, difficult, combative and prideful, and not particularly bright, in Tianati's view. But he kept the dates and controlled the fires with reasonable accuracy.

Tianati arrived at the large earthen circle that served as the village's observatory and greeted the Astronomer, who was standing in front of his home next to the circle.

"I have some news for you," the young Astronomer said, with more than a hint of pomposity. "A bead string has arrived from the People's City. You have been chosen to meet personally with the Chief Astronomer at the Naming ceremony."

Tianati sighed. "You know, Astro, I haven't been home in months. I have been fighting giants. Watching my cousins die. Perhaps you should try it sometime."

The young Astronomer drew back a touch, and puffed his chest and lips at the same time, betraying his displeasure at being challenged and called a diminutive nickname for his important position. "Save your wit for the Chief Astronomer, soldier. If you choose not to go, be assured an escort will be sent to persuade you otherwise."

"Let 'em try. You know, someone has to go talk with the blasted giants about keeping our homes here. You think I trust you to do it?" Tianati turned to go. With his back to the scowling Astronomer, he said quietly, "I'll let you know my decision tomorrow." He walked slowly away.

"You will be ready to leave by the new moon," the astronomer called after him. Tianati let him have the last word and kept walking.

☽ ● ☾

That night Tianati smoked the dream mix he had stayed away from throughout the war. It was a gift from his cousin from way down east on the Petee River. The Petee smokeweed was famous for having great power to bring visions, and also for being a lot of fun to smoke. But for those fighting giants, a night of smoking Petee weed could lead to a very bad day on the battlefield. Tianati had no such worries tonight, and breathed the fired mix in deep. He let himself relax for the first time in months, and his mind began to wander down new paths. He thought of friends he had lost, jokes they had told, and stories they had shared. He thought of women he had loved. The fair skinned Mandan. The Lake Woman with her bewitching songs. The strange, beautiful traveler from the South who had stopped by the soldiers' camp one summer's night, and acted as bold as any warrior. All of them were far away now, if they were even still alive after the chaos of war. As he drifted into sleep, he wondered if it was time to find a nice girl from one of the villages out here on the frontier - a tough, simple girl who could raise beans and sunflower and cook squirrel stew. Or maybe he would meet a sophisticated girl from the People's City, someone who knew the latest stories, someone who knew how to wear her shawl just so, someone who would satisfy his body and his mind. Or perhaps he'd travel far away and find an exotic stranger to bring home . . .

OOO

The Allegh made their home under the stars wherever they gathered to rest with friends. Berengial was home. He sat on a chilled rock, staring up at the stars in the cold night, pondering Didigial's request. *He is correct,* thought Berengial, *someone must travel to the south, bring the news of the "peace" to our kin, and ask for their return. We will need numbers for what will come. But why must it be me?* He was tired in a way he would never admit to his fellow Allegh. Weary of battle and strife.

Pollangial walked up holding two steaming bowls of spiced venison stew and sat down next to Berengial. "Try this. It's delicious. I forgot how good Little cooking was."

Berengial took the stew gratefully and ate in silence, as was the Allegh custom. When they were done, he turned to Pollangial and asked, "How many of the Allegh went south with the Littles when the war started?"

Pollangial mused for several moments. "I know that thirty-two of Vallingal's family, twenty-five of Gherengeral's clan, fifty-two from the south hills, and nearly three hundred from the People's lands made the trek. So at least four hundred, I would say, maybe more. Why?"

"Didigial says that someone has to tell them the war is over."

"Yes, some poor soul." Pollangial smiled a wicked Allegh grin. "I wager that will be you."

"You know I never bet with anyone from the Poll clan."

"Will you need company?

"I have a feeling my company will be selected for me."

"Do you think the Littles suspect our plan?"

"I doubt it, Pollangial. Look, if Didigial chooses me to go south with the message, you must be the one to lead the Allegh. I don't trust Didigial's heart. He's too soft for what must be done. Remember to be swift and hard, and to begin only when you're completely ready, but while they still do not suspect." Berengial paused. "Pollangial, if you have a change of heart, you should follow it. Destruction of their land will only cause our own destruction in due time."

"I don't doubt it, Berengial, but you and I both know there is nothing else to be done. The Littles will try to exterminate us sooner or later. We might as well go down fighting."

Part II

The River

Summer, Year 472

And it is worthy of remark, that the sites selected for settlements, towns, and cities, by the invading Europeans, are often those which were the especial favorites of the mound-builders, and the seats of their heaviest population. Marietta, Newark, Portsmouth, Chillicothe, Circleville, and Cincinnati, in Ohio; Frankfort in Kentucky; and St. Louis in Missouri, may be mentioned in confirmation of this remark. The centres of population are now, where they were at the period when the mysterious race of the mounds flourished.

-Squier & Davis

Ancient Monuments of the Mississippi Valley: Comprising the Results of Extensive Original Surveys and Explorations

FIVE

THE NAMING

Tianati had grumbled to the Astronomer about leaving home, but the truth was he enjoyed travel, and loved the early stages of a journey best of all. A bend in the river several miles below his town brought Point Town into view. He was alone and happy in his boat, a canoe he'd built with his own hands—his fifth canoe—made with hard-earned memories of every flaw discovered through the leans and leaks, flips and sinkings of each of his first four canoes, his hands guided by the remembered instructions of his father, as learned from his forefathers through thousands of failures and successes with thousands of canoes over tens of thousands of years. Old Number Five had travelled with him throughout the war, and bore the marks of several direct hits by giant spears, none of which had affected its worthiness. His travel bag was carefully packed in the waterproof box wedged under the seat, loaded with darts, cutting and butchering tools, fishing line and hooks, sewing needles and thread, resin, a rain hat and spare moks, elk jerky and dried fruit, cooking spices, flint, a raven-shaped stone pipe, and of course several bags of good leaf, including Nokitis' mix. Around his neck he wore a necklace of copper and shells, a message from his town's Astro to the Chief Astronomer. The Astro warned him not to read on penalty of sanction, but of course Tianati had read it as soon as he was out of sight of the town. It was as vapid and pompous

35

as he had suspected, full of puffery and brag: *Over the past three moons I have led the town in increased food production, more rigorous religious observance, and fewer conflicts with the giants. My efforts to more precisely align the observatory have paid dividends, though if I had more workers and supplies I could achieve even greater results.* Tianati thought the Astro was a self-important fool.

The weather was typical of early summer in the northern reaches, wet and cool, but the late spring rains had made the river flow fast and sure, and Tianati made good time. He passed Point Town, pausing only long enough to holler out a greeting to the shore watchmen. Point Town still bustled with a wartime economy, and offered all the distractions and dalliances that former soldiers crave, but Tianati had no time for that now. He looked over his left shoulder as he cruised to the confluence of the Allegh's River and the muddy Crumblebank river that flowed from the mountains to the south, marveling at the densely-packed houses marching up the slopes of Ceremony Hill. *They'll be building on top of the mound next*, he thought. Point Town's Astro had ordered the construction of a large, wide road marching right to the point formed by the two merging rivers. Tianati counted forty-odd long canoes beached where the road entered the river, and thought of the sleepy pre-war village of ten families that had stood here guarding Ceremony Hill just twenty years earlier. Several thousand lived here now; already the elk were scarce. *Too many people*, Tianati mused, *for these wet hills.* He paddled Number Five into the merged flow as the two rivers joined to form the northwest-flowing Ohio and passed by an ancient, looming burial mound, perched on a rocky cliff above the river. The mound was said to be haunted by the spirits of the common ancestors of the giants and the People, and both groups revered, and feared, the site. Tianati bowed his head without even thinking as he passed the spot.

He spent the rest of the day keeping the canoe in the heart of the current. As the light began to fail, he beached his craft at the mouth of the Beaver River, on the edge of Log Town, where his loud-mouthed cousin Gery lived with his abominable family. Unfortunately, duty demanded he stay with Gery and his kids.

In Gery's house, dinner was a raucous, disordered affair. Shouted insults, half-told stories, punches, and loud farts were expected. Occasionally, a brawl would unfold in horrifying fashion. Gery's ten boys and six dogs had been without a mother, or indeed any woman, for as long as any of them could remember, and it showed. Tianati kept hoping Gery would find an older widow in the town and get married, but his manners and his boys' unruliness limited his odds of wooing the fairer sex.

"So Tianati," said Gery with a mouth full of half-chewed meat, "tell us about your glorious battles!" He spat onto the floor. "How many of them oversized pieces of scat did you kill?"

"They were brave fighters, Gery. The pieces of scat are those who stayed safe and fat while the rest of us risked our necks." Tianati knew the night would end in arguing, perhaps even fighting, and thought, *why wait?*

But Gery was too old, fat, and cunning to rise to the bait that easily. "Ha ha!" He belched and lowered his voice. "There's some that say the peace deal was a trick, to get us to put down our arms," he said seriously, "and that they will slit our throats in our sleep once we let the guards retire."

"Better keep one of your brave sons on watch at all times, in that case," said Tianati, not looking up from his food. He continued, "I've heard they bugger you first, by the way, so you may want to keep a jar of bear fat by your bed."

Gery's boys roared, thinking this the best joke they'd heard in years.

Gery didn't laugh this time. "You can make fun all you want, but I don't trust those freaks. This is just a break in the action, that's all. We'll be killing 'em all before too long, or they'll be killing us. Mark my words, mister war hero."

"Maybe, but for all I know I will be a long way from here by the time that happens." Tianati hadn't mentioned the purpose of his trip yet, and hadn't planned on bringing it up at all.

Gery looked at him curiously. "Going somewhere, hero?"

Tianati did not like the sneering way Gery said "hero" - it sounded like a playground taunt. He was starting to think he would have to put Gery in his place before too long. "What business is it of yours where I go, big father?" The kids laughed again, though not as loud. The tension was rising and the boys sensed a fight in the making.

But Gery backed off. He took a swig of juice and rubbed his nose with his arm. "None Tianati, just curious." He turned to one of his sons, who had one hand in the bowl of food and a finger from his other up his nose. "Hey boy, pass me another of those legs, would ya?"

☽ ● ☾

That night Tianati dreamed of a great Observatory Circle, as big as a whole town, that slowly filled with blood. He awoke well before dawn, unrested and with a sore belly. "Damned Gery and his damned dirty food." He dressed and packed, left a small offering of smokeweed, loaded Number Five, and headed back down the Ohio without saying goodbye. He was miles away before the sun was up.

Family obligations behind him, Tianati settled into a pleasant routine of early morning fishing and breakfast, hard paddling for most of the day, and dinner while letting the current take him to sunset, camping in the first dry spot he found. He made great time, and in just a few days the large hilltop ceremonial complex of Muski emerged from behind a bluff on the right bank. Tianati paddled up the swift current of the Muski River to the port, tied up Number Five, and made his way straight to the temple for a prayer. He did not feel particularly religious at the moment, but a prayer had been ringing in his head for the last several days, and he felt it best to get it out so he could sing some silly songs instead. He climbed up the sacred road, knelt at the entrance to the temple, and walked inside. He grabbed a large handful of his best pipe mix, threw it on the ground, and prayed, as he always did, loudly:

Oh spirit that kills, spirit that burns

Lift up the dead, clear out the living

Take my weed, destroy the seed

Turn the world upside down

He paused, not feeling any better. The traditional prayer of sacrifice stuck in his head had come out thin and meaningless, and saying it made him feel no different. Not cleansed. Not forgiven. Not blessed. *All bearscat,* he thought. *Complete scat.* He soon left the temple and returned to the river.

"Just you and me, Number Five," he said aloud to the boat. "No great spirits, no little spirits, no humping spirits at all. Just you and me and a hell of a lot of river to paddle." The boat did not answer.

Tianati filled his canteen at a nearby spring, and started paddling up the Muski to the Great Road. The rainy spring had made the Muski's current strong and hard to row against, and Tianati did not reach the road until the next day.

The Great Road ran from Chillicothe in the west to the Great Observatory and then to the Muski River in the East. Straight and paved, bordered by precise walls, it served as the People's main overland trade and ceremonial route. The paving stones running down the center of the road were chosen for their smoothness, to ease the portage of canoes and cargo sleds. The walls served to mark the road from afar, but also to protect travelers from brigands and, every six or seven years, from the great fires the People set to renew the forests.

Tianati made good time jogging the Great Road. *I will be at the Great Observatory tonight, in plenty of time to see another Naming,* he thought, with a mixture of anticipation and cynicism. The People's most significant annual ceremony was always packed with visitors from around the world, and the week of parties surrounding the Naming itself was marked by an uncomfortable marriage of the sacred and the frivolous. Despite his cynical view of the ceremony itself, Tianati always enjoyed the festivities. He left the road at the first of many gateways to the ceremonial parklands, and camped on the outskirts of the grounds. He slept well for the first time in days.

The Naming Ceremony started three days after Tianati arrived at the Great Observatory. He entered the circle where true names were given along with thousands of others and found a spot in the interior where he could watch the ceremony without too much jostling from the crowd. A fifteen-foot high wall nearly a mile in circumference rose from an inner ditch fifteen feet deep, surrounding thirty acres of flat ground. Near the center of the encircled grounds rose a mound in the shape of a falcon crowned with the Chief Astronomer's quarters. Over a thousand boys and girls, all nineteen years old, stood evenly spaced in a single file line atop the high wall, nearly shoulder to shoulder, silently awaiting their true names. The loud restless throng of spectators in the circle suddenly went silent. Water slowly filled the shallow sandstone-lined channel that ringed the interior of the great circular wall. Haunting flute music rose with the water, and despite his cynicism, Tianati felt his heartbeat quicken and his own excitement rise. Tianati knew he was not the only skeptic among the thousands in attendance for the ceremony. But any skepticism in the audience stayed hidden as the well-honed performance skills of the Astronomers produced the desired effect. Tianati remembered when he had just turned nineteen and stood up on the wall to learn his True Name; how different the ceremony looked from up there, and how different he felt about it all then. The spectacle had seemed sacred, profound to him. Now it seemed cheap and contrived, little more than a well-rehearsed joke re-told again and again. Tianati was skeptical of the ceremony, though he believed in the value of the Post-Naming Missions each youth would receive after the ceremony. The Chief Astronomer would assign to each of them a difficult journey and task. By traveling far away and returning with something, or someone, unique and exotic, they would enrich both themselves and the People. He listened to the murmur of the crowd. Some snippets of conversation came through the din:

"Next year we must bring Uncle Graddel if he's well enough . . ."

"keep your hands out of your nose Droz or we will leave right now . . ."

"the music has never been as good as that year we stood on the wall . . ."

The music stopped all at once. The crowd quieted. The Chief Astronomer rose to the head of the Falcon Mound at the center of the Circle and spoke in a clear, strong voice despite his age. Tianati knew that this Chief Astronomer was from another era. The old guard of the Astronomers believed in the power of the Missions and the importance of bringing new people into the fold, but they were dying off. A new breed of Astronomers who felt that there were too many outsiders diluting the People's culture had began to dominate the ranks, and the giants' revolt had hardened their intolerance. Slavery had even returned to fashion after centuries of disfavor.

The Chief Astronomer had publicly expressed his concern at this narrow, xenophobic view, and he had said that he despaired for the future of the People's civilization. A culture weak from long war and scared of outside influence was a culture in mortal peril, he had declared. The younger Astronomers seemed to disregard his warnings, but for now, at least, he remained Chief, and Tianati hoped that if the old man accomplished nothing else he would do everything in his power to keep intact the fragile peace and open the stagnant eyes and hearts of the People.

The youths on the wall were hundreds of yards from the central mound. Criers stood on smaller mounds at the tail and wing tips of the Falcon Mound and echoed the Chief's words in deep tones for all to hear. To the Chief, it must have sounded like he was in a vast canyon with his own words reverberating back to him. To the assembled thousands in the round flat plain within the encircling walls, it sounded like the Chief was speaking directly to them through his acolytes: "Welcome fellow people in this, the twenty sixth year of the Hawk. This year we celebrate the coming of age of these fine young men and women on the wall with hope and with grief. The wars that have sapped our strength have ended, and our people can once again study and love, play and pray, farm and hunt, and live in peace. But we grieve as well, for those brave ones who died to protect us. They are here with us, though, and they want to dance with us. Lift your voices with me and call them to the circle, call them to the dance, call them to our hearts:

Today we dance throughout the land

The dawn streams over the edge of the world,

south north east west,

light comes to earth, darkness is gone.

beetles, crickets, bats and moths

hurry home to their holes and caves.

The brightest star

shines over the woods,

winking as it sinks and vanishes;

the moon, too, slips to sleep

over the green lawn.

Naming Day has arrived

in the Great Circle;

a new sun lights and an old moon sings

to all who come.

"In just a few moments, we will all watch as the Moon marks the passing of time and reminds us of where we are and when we are. I know that many are becoming skeptical of the meaningfulness of what we gather here to witness."

Tianati knew the Chief Astronomer was speaking to hundreds in the audience, and not to him alone. Nevertheless, he felt as though the eyes of all of the people were on him, accusing him silently of faithlessness. Of soullessness. Of empty death. He wondered who else felt as he did, and whether making all of them feel guilty and fearful was the Chief Astronomer's goal.

"I speak to all of you. Skeptics and believers. Faithful and faithless. Lost and found. The Moon is not alive. You are. The Sun is not a person. You are. The time passes for all of us, no matter the state of our hearts.

"Still, you are with us here tonight. The moon is above you and me equally. And now the moon speaks to us with its grand movement."

A fire appeared at the top of Watch Hill at that moment, signaling that the Astronomers at the Octagon had marked the height of the moon, triggering the start of the official Naming. A cheer went up from the throats of the gathered thousands, and despite his cynicism, Tianati felt his heart well up.

The Chief let the cheers die down. "Tonight, I call on you all without distinction, big and small, Giants and boys, skeptics and believers, slaves and free-peoples, to let your voices join your companions in a song to the coming of the year and the going of the year, to the coming of the night and the going of the night, to the coming of us and the going of us." He led the throngs in the naming song all knew by heart. Tianati sang too. He sang off-pitch and heavy-hearted, but he sang. When the voices died down there was silence. The Chief Astronomer turned in a slow circle, chanting low and steady as he did, pointing with both hands to the young men and women on the wall, who all held unlit torches and now stood with them raised high, waiting. He stopped and gestured to the watchman standing at the rampart that marked the gateway into the giant circle. "Pass the fire!" he cried. The watchman raised a tall, polished wood torch high above him, its flame burning bright blue and white. He echoed the Chief Astronomer: "Pass the fire!" and touched his flame to the torch of the young man who stood at the end of the line of young people atop the wall. When the young man's torch burst into flames, the Chief Astronomer called out his true name and gave him his Mission. The flames were spread from person to person along the wall-top, each earning a true name with the lighting of the torch, and each learning where their Mission would take them. Some would go far to the north to gather copper; some to the distant oceans to the south and east for shells; some to the western mountains for black obsidian; and some to exotic tribes for seeds, songs and interesting people. After a few hours, a ring of bright fire crowned the ceremonial circle, the flames' reflection gleaming off the ring of water on the inside of the wall. Another generation had joined the ranks of named People. The throng on the circle floor erupted in cheers.

When it was all over, Tianati found himself walking towards the Falcon Mound, towards the Chief Astronomer, as the old man held informal prayer sessions with bold attendees brave enough or foolish enough to approach the Chief Astronomer without invitation. The Astronomer entertained them, treating each as a special case, and Tianti hung back without speaking. Finally the Chief Astronomer turned to him.

"I know you, Tianati. I know your task. You must come with me." The Chief turned and walked back down the mound towards his house – the only house permitted in the whole of the Great Observatory compound. Tianati paused only a moment before following him, as he knew he must. An invitation to pass through the doors of the Chief Astronomer's home could not be refused, though it would likely change one's life.

Berengial enjoyed the play of firelight on the water and the strange Naming songs of the Littles, and thought of how different the big circle looked filled with celebrating masses instead of the handful of frightened priests he'd encountered a few months ago. Throughout the Naming ceremony he snacked on various festival foods he'd gathered outside the grounds: deep-fried squirrel legs, roasted spiced nuts of every variety, popped corn, sunflower seeds, elk jerky. *They really are better with food than we are*, he thought.

When the ceremony was over he felt sleepy and started to head for his tent. Just then a Little priest ran up to him, out of breath and sweaty.

"There you are," he breathed. "The Chief Astronomer respectfully requests your presence in his home. I would be pleased to lead the way, if you will follow."

"Lead on, little one."

☽ ● ☾

Tianati was surprised by how humble and normal the house was. A bag of smokeweed hung from a hook on the wall. A simple woven rug and a small ceremonial fire were all that adorned the swept floor. The Chief sat on a chair fashioned from cypress and elk antlers. He motioned for Tianati to sit in an identical chair across the fire. Tianati politely offered some of his weed to the fire, and made a gesture of offering some more to the Chief. The Chief laughed and said, "Keep it Tianati, you are likely to have more need of good smoke than I for some time to come!" He grinned with the mischievous, twinkling eyes of a boy. "Try some of this instead. It is a recipe passed down from Chief to Chief for over two hundred years. Supposed to make you smarter."

He handed Tianti a pouch of smokeweed. Tianati took a small pinch of the weed and packed it into the bowl of his raven pipe. He pulled a long sliver of wood from his pack, extended it into the fire for a light, and held it just above the bowl, pulling in his breath with a combination of excitement and suspicion. *These are the guys running things, and they think smoking makes you smarter,* he thought, *but I suppose they could be on to something, since everyone treats them like gods. Besides, it tastes good.*

Tianati did not rest on formality. He went right to the point. "Why have you chosen me, Chief, and what have you chosen me for?"

The Chief laughed again, and took a drag from his own pipe. "We read all the reports from the battlefields, you know. You are known as a tough fighter, a respected leader, and an irredeemable skeptic. You have also been accused, or lauded, depending on your point of view, for being a defender of the Allegh."

Tianati wondered to himself how he had developed a reputation as a skeptic. Aloud, he said, "I've killed as many giants as any soldier, Chief. But I don't see the Allegh as all that different from us. Hell, they're better fighters. We're just more numerous and better armed."

"No doubt Tianati, no doubt. As enjoyable as it would be for us to spend the night talking about politics and war, I called you here for a different reason. I need you to deliver a message."

"I am not a courier, Chief, with all due respect. Don't you have legions of runners whose only job it is to sprint down the roads with bead messages? I passed three of them on my trip from the Muski to here alone!"

"There are no roads that go where this message must go, or at least no roads of the People. And this is no bureaucratic message detailing the fire-starting strategy. No, Tianati. I need you to go to the ancient home of our ancestors down south, to tell whatever kin of ours still survive that the war has ended and they can come home. I need you to go to the City of the Gods in Zialand."

The name evoked childhood stories of great stone pyramids and jaguars stalking through lush forests, half mythical tales of exodus, and a memory of kin left behind millennia ago. Some of those kin had eventually migrated to the north, but many were rumored to remain in the great cities of Zialand, thousands of miles to the south. The giants, too, had legends of coming from Zialand. When the war broke out in earnest many of the People and giants who chose not to fight went together to the south to try to find their lost kin and settle there. Tianati had always assumed they were all dead.

"They are not dead," said the Chief, as if he read Tianati's mind, "no, they are not dead. We need them to return to complete the reconciliation. We need them to return to renew our moribund polity. You must go to them, and bring those who will come home, home."

Tianati allowed this to sink in. He supposed he wasn't getting a break any time soon. "I will need some companions. I should take a regiment, perhaps my old regiment from the war."

"No," the Chief said, "that is not the way it must be. You will not go alone, however. You will take a strong companion. Ahh, here he is now!"

Tianati turned to look at the door. Over seven feet of muscle and oversized bone stooped to enter the small house. "Greetings Allegh!" the Chief exclaimed. The Chief could not use the giant's name because he did not know it. Giants never shared their names with any non-Alleghs.

"Hello Chief," said the giant as quietly as a giant could.

"This is a joke? A test of some sort?" Tianati asked, looked incredulously at the Chief. "I am to travel several thousand miles with none but a giant beside me? I will not make it to the ocean without getting my head ripped off, either by this one or the brother of some poor soul this one's kin have killed."

The giant smiled. "You might not make it to the door of this fine house without getting your head ripped off with that attitude."

Tianati glared at the Allegh, but before he could fire off a retort, the Chief spoke to the giant. "Take a seat Allegh, anywhere you'd like. I fear my chairs will not fit you."

"The floor is well suited for me," he said, sitting as far from Tianati as could be managed in the small room. "Chairs are for Chiefs and women. Which are you?" he asked, smiling at Tianati.

The Chief broke in again before Tianati could get a word out. "You two are going to take the message; it has already been decided by the Allegh leader and the People's Council. There will be no debate, and there will be no fighting between the two of you. Tianati, a giant must go, to convince the Allegh in Zialand to return. He will also be good in a fight, as I'm sure you must know."

"I fear that will be my problem," Tianati said.

OOO

Berengial looked at the Little sitting on the chair next to the Chief Astronomer. Cocky little punk, he thought. Berengial thought of the instructions Didigial had given him the day before.

"Go with the Little to the great city in the heart of Zialand in the south and find our exiles," Didigial had told him. "The Littles think you'll merely be delivering a message of peace and joy, and that the return of the exiles will help secure the peace we fought so hard for. You know what you must do. My instincts tell me things may be very different than we hope in Zialand. Be prepared to encounter great hardship and suffering among our kin. You must help them in whatever way you can. We'll need their numbers."

"I will do what one Allegh can do," Berengial replied. He did not say it as a signal of limitation. He said it as a show of power. "In my absence you must let Pollangial show you the way to go forward here." Even though Didigial was the Allegh leader in name, Berengial meant it as a command.

$$\text{☽ ● ☾}$$

The Chief told Tianati and the giant to spend the next few days enjoying the post-Naming festivities and getting acquainted with each other while his attendants prepared provisions for them. The next morning, Tianati and the giant ate a big breakfast and walked around to take in the sights. Tianati wondered how this festival looked to the giant, a man who preferred sleeping under open skies in empty country. Thousands of the People milled about, gathered from across a continent, many having waited their entire lives for the chance to come and be a part of the Naming. They clustered in camps set at respectful distances from the octagonal walled plaza. Within hailing distance of Tianati alone, over a hundred of the People were encamped.

A large group of Kan Tuk People had made the easy journey from the rich lands to the south, dressed to show their wealth: finely-trimmed trousers and elaborate heron-feathered headgear on the men, beautiful red- and blue-dyed woven skirts and well-polished pearl necklaces on the women. The Kan Tuks were known to be exceptionally pious, and certainly thought of themselves as the most devout of the People. They were usually among the better represented groups at the Naming and, befitting their own sense of piety and priority, their camps were generally placed closest to the ceremonial complex. Their fine travel huts were lined up in neat rows less than a mile from the sacred earthen walls.

Nearby, a smaller group of Lake People from the lands to the north had made their camp. They had come mostly by canoe, with just a short overland portage to slow their trip. Their children were the most eye-catching members of their camp, clothed only in brightly-colored paints and oils. Their heads were bright blue and their feet were painted bright red, and their torsos were covered in mixed orange and green like the leaves of the early fall forest.

A dozen Buffalo People dressed in brown leather accented with panther-tooth spikes sat around a fire pit a stone's throw behind the Kan Tuk camp. Beyond them, traders of indeterminate origin sat before garish overhangs festooned with flags and rattles. To one side of the Lake People's camp a pipe maker hawked his specialty — a black stone owl pipe with eyes of rare blue rock mined far away in the southwest. Several flint-workers were seated at a row of temporary tables set up just behind the fresh-water spring, carefully chipping away at their work. Nearby, a gaudy coastal shell-man adorned in a yellow canary-feather shawl chanted sea songs, surrounded by baskets of shells. Everywhere families browsed and chatted, many snacking on roasted corn or deliciously spiced meat-on-a-stick.

"Over here, giant," said Tianati, gesturing to an inconspicuous yellow tent beyond the flint-workers. "Let me show you the best of the festival."

"Is that where the women can be had?"

"No, something far less troublesome." They walked over to the yellow tent and Tianati waved politely to the small old man sitting cross-legged before it. "Would you be able to recommend a good travel mix, sir?"

"First let me see if I remember your taste correctly, young buck. You are the warrior who curses his atlatl, the hunter who spares the bear, the wanderer who loves his home, the smoker who goes by the name Tianati?"

"I'm not sure I would put it just that way, mixer, but yes, I am Tianati. I saw you last at my sister's Naming, many years ago. I'm leaving soon on a long and uncertain journey. What can you do to ease my travel?"

"Please come in and have a seat. I will find the best mix for you." The old man stood slowly and ducked into his tent. The giant looked at Tianati questioningly.

"Come on in, giant, if you can fit." They went into the small tent and sat on the floor, the giant hunched forward so his head wouldn't touch the roof of the tent. The old man was up on his knees picking through bundles of dried leaf that hung in bags from the tent's cross bars. He pulled small amounts from seven different bags, and then a larger bunch from a bluish bag hanging higher than the rest. He put all the leaf in a small, four-legged, frog-headed bowl in the middle of the tent, and tossed the contents like a salad for several minutes, pausing every few seconds to take a deep smell of the mix. At one point he reached back into the high blue bag and grabbed a smaller bunch of smokeweed to add to the bowl. He then paused before saying a prayer and singing a jaunty tune. He stood and reached into a hidden fold near the top of his tent, his hand emerging as a tightly closed fist. He closed his eyes just as tightly, lowered his voice, and chanted in a language Tianati did not know while letting a fine brown powder slowly spill from his opening fist into the bowl. Tianati looked at the giant's face as the old man worked and watched the Allegh's bemusement change into fascination.

"Do you have a fresh bag?" The old man's voice was back to normal. Tianati reached into his pack and pulled out a leather leaf pouch. He opened the corded top as wide as it would go. The old man mixed the leaf in the bowl one last time, grabbed a solid handful, and carefully put the leaf into Tianati's pouch.

Tianati put the mix to his nose and took a deep whiff, saying a brief prayer as he breathed out. "Amazing."

"And now you're going to go and burn it all up, aren't you? What's the point of that?" the giant said.

The old man laughed. "What's the point of anything?"

Indeed, thought Ti.

OOO

Berengial went to sleep that night with the smell of the smokeweed still in his nostrils. He would later blame the strange dreams of the night on the weed's fumes. When he was a child his own grandfather had mixed medicines in much the same way that the old Little mixed smokeweed; the two old men would probably have had much to talk about. Berengial could hear the sound of his grandfather's voice inside his head as he drifted into sleep. "Berengial, always trust and doubt your elders. Trust that we know something, but doubt that we know everything. Always doubt and trust yourself. Doubt that you have learned all there is to learn. Trust that you have learned enough to do what you must do now. But never trust the Littles. Some can be tolerated. But eventually they will succumb to the smallness of their minds, and turn on us." The memory of his grandfather's advice gave him small comfort and his sleep remained troubled.

SIX

THE PEOPLE'S CITY

The Chief gave Tianati and the Giant a parting blessing, and told them to go to the People's City, two days downriver, where the Council would give them a bead string with the message for the exiles. Tianati reluctantly left Number Five behind in favor of a flatboat large enough to carry himself, the giant, and all their provisions. They had to pull the flatboat by rope down the creek that led out of the Great Observatory grounds, each walking on opposite sides of the creek on well-tended paths kept for just that purpose. The day was uncommonly hot for early summer, and there was no wind. The giant clearly did not enjoy the heat. His pride would not let him complain, but his face betrayed his discomfort. Tianati started whistling an old marching tune.

"Cut that foolishness out," mumbled the giant. Tianati stopped whistling the march, and then started on a jaunty old smoking song. Without warning, the Giant yanked his rope hard, pulling Tianati into the creek. "I warned you," he yelled, between giant-sized guffaws. Tianati pulled the giant's rope as hard as he could, hoping to catch him off-balance and return the favor. The giant hardly budged, and just laughed harder. Tianati found himself laughing despite himself, stopping only when a courier racing up-creek looked down at him disapprovingly, and bursting out in laughter again as the giant glared threateningly at the courier, causing him to scoot down the road with startled speed.

That night, as they camped together where the creek emptied into the Ohio River, Tianati looked downriver and said, "You know, giant, we're probably going to die on this little trip of ours."

"Oh, I know. But one way or the other, we will die someday. Might as well be while we're doing something worthwhile."

"You think this mission is worthwhile?

The giant paused, as if searching for just the right words. "If the return of the exiles helps prevent another war, it will have been worth it."

"There will always be another war, giant. You know that."

"The more distant that day, the better."

Tianati said nothing more. He smoked the first of the new travel leaf, and fell into a sleep without dreams.

$$\text{)} \bullet \text{(}$$

The flatboat felt fat and bloated after piloting old Number Five for years. *The City is not too far*, Tianati thought. *We can switch to a better boat for the long journey downriver.* A decade ago, on his Mission, Tianati had used a specially built longboat to go from the People's City to the great forks, where he traded for a canoe to head up towards the mountains. He knew the value of the longboat: comfortable, steerable, and yet still capable of carrying lots of cargo. With the giant to help paddle and steer, a longboat was the superior downriver boat for the amount of provisions they would need for the months' long voyage.

Tianati thought about what else they could find at the City. The women. He wondered how the giant would be received in the districts of the City on the Kan Tuk side of the Ohio, where the women were willing. He looked at the giant sitting quietly in the very middle of the boat. *He is not comfortable in the water.* Tianati leaned suddenly to one side, tilting the boat, and laughed as the giant slapped his hands down to grab hold of the sides and steady himself, cursing loudly.

OOO

Berengial hated boats. They were necessary for some travel, but he despised the powerlessness he felt as the damned crafts drifted on unseen eddies and swirling currents. He was also a poor swimmer. He tried to stay as close to the center of the cursed boat as he could, and moved as little as possible. He nearly tore the Little's head off when he rocked the boat. But his anger and discomfort vanished when the boat rounded a bend and he saw the People's City for the first time.

Nothing he'd seen before prepared him for what he saw now. A soaring bridge of rope and wood crossed the expansive breadth of the Ohio River, leaping from stone piling to stone piling in seven spans. On the south bank, the bridge turned to a walled road that ran up to a flattened promontory. There, a tower built from five stacked stone cylinders rose higher than any structure Berengial had encountered. The top of the tower glowed with an intense blue-white fire that was clearly visible even in the brightness of the summer's day, announcing the seat of the People's power: the Council.

On the north bank of the Ohio River, a network of roads spiderwebbed outward from the bridge's landing. Berengial saw countless houses and buildings of unknown purpose, and several of the People's game courts. He could see smoke rising from cooking fires burning on street corners and in homes throughout the city, and people were crossing the bridge in great numbers going in both directions, bustling about on unknown business. *So this is a City,* he thought.

Tianati poled the flatboat to the main north bank landing, just past the bridge. Twelve eager porters helped beach the craft and carried the supplies to a wooden warehouse at the top of the landing. Tianati tossed them a small bag of smokeweed with a smile.

"See if you can find us a solid longboat. We'll trade this flatboat for one suitable for a trip all the way downriver." He turned to the giant. "Come on, let's find a place to stay."

"Can't we just camp somewhere outside of the City?"

"You won't want to do that, trust me." He led the giant through a maze of side streets to the main road over the bridge. The giant marveled at the engineering the People had used to span the river. At the end of each span, two stripped white pine trunks fifty feet tall had been driven deep into the ground on either side of the road. Long strands of tightly-woven rope were secured to the tops of the pine poles on either end of each span, and hung down in the middle like two long smiles flanking the path. Smaller ropes were tied to the long ropes and hung straight down, where they secured the flat planks that formed the bridge over the river.

The giant looked at the structure skeptically before stepping onto it. "I suppose if it can support hundreds of you Littles it can hold one giant," he said.

"This has held up for over a hundred years. Every day it is tested and cleaned and repaired. See those five men on the second span over there?" Tianati pointed to a group clustered around the base of one of the pine poles on the second span. "They're making sure the pole is still sound. If there's any doubt, they'll install a new one in a matter of days. They don't hunt or fight, and all their food is given to them. All they do is tend the bridge."

"Some life," mused the giant.

"They love it. Their fathers did it, and their fathers before them. They hold it as the highest of honors." As they crossed the span, Tianati felt a sense of pride as he imagined how impressive the bridge must be to the giant. When they stepped off onto the opposite bank, however, his pride turned to shame. On either side of the path, spikes topped with gruesome severed Allegh heads stared down at them, the noses removed in disrespect – the People knew that the Allegh believed the most ancient part of a man's spirit was expressed in the nose. Tianati looked at the giant. The People's preparations for peace with the giants had not yet included taking down the macabre display, but if the Allegh was bothered by it he did not let it show. Tianati decided to say nothing.

Just down the road from the bridge they stopped at a small prayer temple. Tianati said a perfunctory prayer while the giant stood quietly to the side. "If I remember correctly," Tianati said more to himself than the giant, "we will find the Girls' House down near the bottom of that hill." He led the giant to a side street that sloped down to the river.

"Girls' house? You stay in a girls' house?" They stopped at a crossroads.

"Just stick with me, big guy." Tianati took the road to the right, made another left onto a dirt path, and stopped in front of a long, low, wooden structure showing little sign of occupation.

"Looks like no one's home," the giant said.

Tianati did not answer. He rapped his knuckles on the frame of thick logs that braced the main doorway, paused, then rapped again. Curtains rustled somewhere inside the door and a petite old lady with coal-black hair appeared, smiling. "Would you like to stay in the Girls' House?" she asked.

Tianati smiled back. "Can you take care of a giant, too?"

The old lady's smile broadened. "Of course! Come on in."

Tianati motioned for the giant to follow him into the low structure. The Allegh looked reluctant, but ducked and followed.

Berengial wondered what foolishness the Little had in store for him. The old lady led them into the house. Berengial was surprised to see that the house was little more than a large shed designed solely to conceal the opening to a deep cavern that descended into the hillside. Lit torches were attached to the sides of the cavern, and the way was surprisingly smooth and easy to navigate. After having to duck slightly at the cave's entrance, Berengial could walk fully upright. The old lady led them to a soaring space where the cavern roof arched thirty feet overhead. Bizarre crystalline drippings of earth formed columns throughout the room. Into this otherworldly realm an impossible structure of thin wood and cloth had been built, with platforms wedged between the crystal columns and ladders dropped here and there to create a cave warren. But Berengial's eye was drawn to the denizens more than the structures of this subterranean den; several lovely young women smiled out at him from behind their colorful curtains.

"This place is sacred," said the old lady. "This cave has been a place of high spirits for thousands of years. We've found that Xanach — the spirit of love — is particularly strong here. Worship well!"

Tianati smiled at the giant and climbed up a nearby ladder at the invitation of a brown-haired beauty behind a green and blue curtain. Berengial thought he was better off staying close to the floor. Fortunately, a girl with long raven hair beckoned for him to join her behind her red curtain on the ground floor. She gestured for him to lie back on pillows stuffed with soft straw.

Allegh women were matter-of-fact about sex. They got down to business quickly and wasted little time on the act itself. Berengial was unprepared for the Little woman's long, slow approach to lovemaking. First she kissed his neck and ears with her tiny lips, with a touch so soft and gentle that Berengial wasn't sure whether some of her kisses were merely breaths. Meanwhile her fingers deftly removed his breechcloth and began toying with his hard member. She smiled and giggled at its size, cooing with pleasure in his ears. She took her time moving her kisses down his expansive chest, while her hand began to grasp and pull his hardness. Then she kissed the swollen purple head, taking it into her mouth, swirling her tongue around its crown. Berengial gasped. He'd never felt anything remotely like this before. The girl sat up and smiled. She propped herself up on her knees and slowly, teasingly, lowered herself onto him. She could not go down all the way, but she bounced up and down on the end of its length with obvious pleasure until Berengial felt himself exploding into her with the force of the river itself. She laughed, but didn't stop bouncing, until he found himself rising yet again.

)●(

The next day they stumbled out of the Girls' House into the bright sunlight of mid-day, satisfied, tired, and very hungry. "Let's find some good spiced stew," said Tianati. "I think there used to be a place by the river that was pretty good." He led the giant back down towards the river, not far from the bridge, then turned downstream along the riverside road, passing a large ballcourt where teams were practicing before a sparse crowd of bored onlookers.

The giant had a smile on his face. "You remember that word the old lady in the girls' house said: 'Xanach'?"

"Yes. It's an old word, hardly spoken anymore except at stuffy ceremonies."

"Funny thing," said the giant, "we have the same word in our high Allegh language. It's what we say at the consecration of a new marriage, and at the birth of a child." He was silent for a while as they meandered through the streets. Slowly, the giant said, "So I suppose the myths might be true. Maybe your people and our folk have a common ancient history after all. A time when we shared 'Xanach'."

"We share something else too, apparently," said Tianati. "A love of women."

"And of food," said the giant, changing the subject. Something about their conversation, maybe the talk of a shared heritage, seemed to trouble him. "Which reminds me, where's this place with the good stew, anyway? I'm starving."

"Ahh, there it is." Tianati started walking to a ragged lean-to with a large pit fire in the back. A tripod supported an enormous steaming cauldron over the fire. A boy of about ten stirred the pot slowly, wiping his brow every once in awhile. The smell was fantastic, a strong savory smell of many roasted and stewed meats, blended with a woody scent and a sharp heady spice that slightly stung the eyes. Tianati's mouth watered. "Two bowls, please," he said. He handed one to the giant, along with a spoon from a rack near the tripod, and started eating his own almost immediately.

The giant sniffed at the stew, then started in himself, eating quickly and with obvious relish. "I think we stopped fighting so we could eat your Little food again," he said through bites. "What can we expect from your Council today?"

"I'm not sure. I've never appeared before the Council. The Chief Astronomer said they would give us the message beads and a good map string. I suppose they may also want to impart to us the importance of not screwing this up."

"I doubt we'll ever see this land again. The stories I have heard of the lands to the south are not at all comforting."

"I'm told it's so vast and varied that you can find almost anything," Tianati said. "Great cities, expansive wilderness, lost kin, deadly new enemies. I haven't been far south. For my Mission I traveled west a great distance to the high rocky mountains. I was told to bring back as much obsidian as I could carry, and as many talented people as I could find. I came to realize how small and cozy our world around the Ohio River is. You cannot imagine the sheer size of the horizon on the great plains. The bison run in herds so thick and numerous they look like a muddy lake flooding in a storm. Towns dot the plains, some with women as beautiful as spirits, others with people as vicious as snakes."

"I can see the usefulness of the obsidian. It makes a good blade and tool. But why were you told to bring back people? Aren't there already too many people here?" The giant gestured across the city spreading up both banks of the river.

"The Council decided hundreds of years ago that numbers didn't matter. We need fresh blood, new ideas, creative people to keep our land in harmony and alive. At the Naming Ceremony, each young person is told where to go and what to bring back. Everyone brings something material. Those with the right talents are also asked to seek out bright minds and nimble hands, pretty faces and strong backs, sweet singers and skilled storytellers. In that way we strengthen the People. We also improve our relations with the other peoples of the world. But there are many now who question whether we should be inviting so many new people in, and who think there are too many people on the land. I tend to be old fashioned on this point; I say let them come."

"Why would these people leave their homes to travel thousands of miles with a complete stranger to a new land?"

"Ah ha – that is why only some of us are chosen for this part of the Mission. I can be very persuasive. I can tell people what they need to hear. Those who feel their talents are not appreciated, those who have a need for a great adventure like in the old tales, those who have not been accepted in their own tribes or families—they can all be persuaded. Once I met a young man in a high mountain village who had built his own flute, a slight instrument with a high, peculiar sound. His family hated it. They mocked him and forbade him from using it around people.

He would climb up distant crags alone just to make his own strange music. He returned to the land of the People with me and now makes hundreds of these flutes a year. He lives in a large town north of here, near a stand of ash trees; apparently the wood of the ash makes particularly good instruments. He has six children by three women, and is quite happy. Do you remember the haunting final song at the Naming ceremony? His flutes made it sound uniquely beautiful."

"You're a strange bunch." The giant finished the last of his stew. Somehow, Tianati had finished first. They both took a second bowl for the road, and started up the hill towards the Council's tower.

OOO

Berengial ran his hands along the smooth walls of the road to the Council Tower, marveling at the craftsmanship. The road rounded the edge of the bluff over the river to face the tower. He had never seen a structure quite like it. Five levels of neat, circular walls had been built from polished sandstone, and each level was roofed over with heavy beams. He wondered how hard it would be to tear it down.

The entrance was framed by two leaning timbers pointing up like a giant arrowhead. Perfectly straight wooden staffs topped with copper-plated pinecones, the symbols of illumination adopted as the emblems of the People's Council, flanked the opening. Inside, a basket of fire was suspended above the center of the large, open floor, so high even the giant could walk under it without fear. Even higher up, a wooden platform jutted inward from the wall. On this platform were benches of hewn log, well worn by the buttocks of councilors from centuries past; Berengial could just barely make out the feet of a group of councilors seated there now, as well as ladders leading up to hidden rooms and more platforms.

On the ground level, in front of Tianati and Berengial, was a larger, flat-topped platform. A junior Astronomer robed in white led Berengial and Tianati up the steep stairs to the platform, then went down himself to some hidden alcove. From their vantage on top of the platform, Berengial could just make out the councilors' faces where they sat in a half circle behind the large hanging fire basket.

Tianati greeted the Council. "Hallo Councilors! We come at your request!"

An elder councilor to Berengial's left answered in a thin, reedy voice. "Welcome! Please sit." Berengial and Tianati sat cross-legged on the platform's smooth floor. Berengial could still just see the faces over the flames, though he guessed Tianati could not. He saw that all of the councilors appeared to be women.

A louder voice boomed from the center of the circle of councilors. "You whom we will not name out of respect have been an important part of the peace we have reached. Do you value its preservation?"

Berengial knew she was addressing him, as he would not have allowed any Little to use his real name. "I would not have come if I did not."

"And you, Tianati, you have already made great journeys and fought many battles. Are you prepared for an even longer and more dangerous mission?"

"I will do what must be done, Councilor."

"Very well. We have prepared a bead string bearing the message of the Council. You are to deliver the message to all of the exiled People and Allegh in the City of the Gods in Zialand. You will, if you are able, help any who wish to return to make the journey home. Tianati, you should employ whatever skills of persuasion you have learned to bring as many home as possible. The People and the Allegh who fled to Zialand are those among each folk who lived well together. Some even married, I am told. Their example is our best chance of preserving the peace. More importantly, having driven them away with our war, it is our duty to tell them they may come home to a peaceful land. To aid your travels, we have prepared a map string for you with the best information available on the route. Your fastest way will be down the river to Mouth City, then across the great sea to Zialand. The roads are excellent in Zialand, but the politics are in turmoil. Tread with care."

"We will do our best, Councilor."

Berengial swallowed hard. *The great sea?* He did not like the sound of that one bit.

$$\text{☾ ● ☾}$$

The junior Astronomer escorted them back down the stairs. When they reached the archway, he placed two bead strings around Tianati's neck. The first was made mostly of copper, with bits of shell and polished stone. The Astronomer told them this was the message. The second had a good deal more shell, and lots of turquoise, a rare blue stone Tianati had only seen once before, on his Mission to the western mountains. The Astronomer said this was the map, and took some time showing Tianati how to read it. Finally, he handed Tianati a bag filled with useful items to trade. "Use these as you see fit. But when you get to Zialand, they will be less useful. Down there they use a bean as a measure of trade, and are not likely to accept our items as anything of value. Look for People's homes along the way. You will find pockets of us everywhere along your route. Another thing. Take this." He handed Tianati a copper tube stopped with wood at both ends. "When you get to Zialand, spread the balm inside this tube on your nose and shoulders."

"Why? Does it keep flies away?"

The Astronomer looked at him with a small smile. "Do you know where the name 'Zialand' comes from?"

"No, I've only heard it in old men's stories."

"The desert folk of the far west named it – it is the country directly to their south. Zia is their word for sun. They named it the Land of the Sun. The cream in this tube will help keep your northern skin from getting burned by the strong southern sun." The Astronomer turned and called back into the chamber, "Naamani!"

Tianati put the tube in his pack and wondered what else he would learn on this trip. He saw a young woman emerge from the darkness of the council chamber, her hair cut short in the fashion of slaves, but her eyes flashing bold, flecked with green-hazel spokes. She bowed to the Astronomer. "Yes, sir."

The Astronomer turned to Tianati. "The Council has ordered Naamani to accompany you. Keep her with you until your mission is completed. She can cook and clean and, though small, carry some loads. She is excellent with dogs, and will manage two good dogs for you." He turned back to the slave. "Go to the pen and pick the best two you can find. Gather enough provisions for you and the dogs to last you a month." He looked at Tianati. "Where will you camp tonight?"

"We were hoping to eat well, so I thought we'd be outside near the food vendors on the north bank."

"Very well. Naamani, find their camp and join them before dawn. You now belong to them."

Tianati turned to her with a wry smile. "I don't believe we've been properly introduced. I am Tianati, and this big man is a giant who refuses on principle to ever divulge his name to tiny little folks like us."

She did not smile, but did not avert her gaze. "Yes, sir."

The giant shrugged. "Make sure you pick dogs that don't bite giants, will you?" he said.

Tianati laughed. "Among the many unpleasant things you will learn about giants on this trip, Naamani, is that they hate dogs."

☽●☾

That night they slept in a cleared field not far from the concentration of food vendors where they had found dinner, or more accurately, dinners. The food had been so good they had sampled offerings from three different cooks.

"Giant," Tianati said suddenly, as they lay on their backs near the dying fire, staring up into the sky, "do you see that constellation up there that looks like a large man with three bright stars in his belt, and wide shoulders? You know what we call that, don't you?"

"You call it 'The Giant Warrior.' That is well known to us. And the big scooper over there you call 'The Pipe.' You Littles are always so creative." Sarcasm was an Allegh specialty.

"What do the Allegh call the Giant Warrior?"

The giant paused, as if considering whether he should share this part of Allegh lore with the Little. Finally, in a quiet voice, he said, "He is a giant to us too. But one with a name, and a story." Tianati stayed quiet, wanting to hear the story, if the giant was willing to tell it. After a while of waiting in silence, his eyes drooped shut and he began to doze. He thought he heard the giant singing in a low, sad voice and in a strange tongue as he began to slip into deep unconsciousness, remembering as he fell asleep that giants did not tell stories, they only sang them.

SEVEN

THE FALLS

They woke before dawn. The bloated feeling from too much feasting had passed, and both Tianati and the giant were hungry. During the night, the slave girl Naamani had joined the camp, and when Tianati awoke she had several sticks of fresh spiced meat roasting over a fire for breakfast and good hot atsik brewing. Her dogs sat watchfully at the edge of the camp. She tossed a few choice pieces to each. "Here you go Pug. Good dog Huk." The dogs' tails wagged appreciatively.

Tianati watched her feed the dogs as he packed a morning pipe with the mix he had picked up outside the Great Observatory. He offered it politely to the giant, thinking the Allegh would again refuse. He was surprised when the giant took the pipe.

"Can you give me a light?" he asked, through a crooked grin. Tianati hesitated only a moment before striking his flint rock near his firebrand. He cupped his hand to protect the small flame and leaned over to light the pipe.

"May earth carry you to the sky," he said politely. He looked at the giant curiously. "What changed?"

"I figured it was rude to keep refusing. I suppose you wore me down with all your requests. Anyway, am I supposed to feel different?"

"Give it a moment, and stop trying to feel something. Think about the river we have ahead of us."

"I suppose we'll reach the falls later today."

"It seems likely. Stand up." Tianati stood and motioned for the giant to do the same. The giant took his time, and swayed unsteadily once he reached his feet. Naamani watched him through curious eyes while she packed up her cooking gear and provisions.

"I hope I can paddle," the giant said. "I suppose you get used to feeling like your head is full of air?"

"You stop feeling like that and just notice a little . . . enhancement, a little more awareness of your place in things. That sounds strange, I know, but it just seems to open up my eyes—my mind—a little more."

"Whatever you say, boss. Maybe your open eyes or mind or whatever can help us see the falls before we tumble over them." He pulled the longboat out of the brush and dragged it to the edge of the river, tossing in his bedroll and pack. "You coming?"

OOO

Berengial thought he would throw up from the despicable weed smoke. But he would be damned if he showed that kind of weakness to the Littles. He focused on keeping the longboat in the center of the current. The river was narrowing and picking up speed, and he could tell they were approaching the rapids, a series of short but intense falls that a skilled boater could negotiate in a canoe. He and Tianati had decided to ride them out rather than drag the heavy boat and all the supplies down the long Falls Path. They had strapped and tied everything down as securely as possible. Despite his better judgment, Berengial had sat towards the front of the longboat. Tianati had instructed, "The stronger paddler should be in the front; it will make it easier for me to steer well from the back." Berengial thought he saw a hint of a smile at the corners of the Little's mouth. Naamani sat in the middle, with the dogs lying down by her feet.

At first, Berengial treated the river as an enemy, battling stones and fighting the current. With sheer strength and force of will he kept the longboat upright and pointing downriver. Tianati laughed as Berengial thrust his paddle into a boulder as if to pierce its rocky heart. "Go with the river, giant, don't combat it." Berengial decided to listen, and started to let the river make his choices, pushing the longboat in the direction the river wanted to take it, letting the current come to him. He felt like laughing himself as he fell into a relationship with the river, giving what was asked and taking what it offered. He heard Tianati call out to him from the back of the boat over the din of rushing water, "Hang on, it's about to get rough!"

The river started dropping out from under them, sending the long-boat plunging down at uncomfortable speed. The companionable relationship Berengial had developed with the rushing water was quickly beginning to sour. He instinctively resorted to his fighting frame of mind, desperately thrusting and parrying with his paddle.

"Easy giant, don't oversteer!"

But Berengial could not stop fighting for his life. He pushed with all his strength off a smooth boulder rushing towards him, but the paddle slipped and he plunged headlong into the rushing foam. The roar of the river went silent and he remembered nothing more.

Tianati tried to slow the longboat while he searched for a sign of the giant. The Allegh had gone straight under, and Tianati had seen only a glimpse of wet clothing that surfaced briefly thirty feet down-river, and then nothing. Tianati heard the voice of his grandfather in his head, talking to him on the banks of a rushing river far to the north. *Bodies move differently than boats do. If you ever get tossed out, hold your breath until you are released. Cover your head so the rocks don't knock you out. The river will spit you up somewhere, don't worry.* He made his decision before he even knew it had been made. "Paddle hard to the right bank!" he yelled to Naamani, then took a deep breath, jumped feet-first into the river, held onto the boat just long enough to push it hard towards the slower current near the right bank, and let the boat go with the girl. He wrapped his hands over his head, took a deep breath, and hoped his grandfather had been right.

OOO

Berengial awoke to a prickly pain in his neck. He saw tall pines overhead and smelled damp wood reluctantly burning. He sat up on one elbow and brushed pine needles from the back of his neck. Tianati was sitting by the fire, skinning some small animal.

"Back from the dead?" the Little said.

"What happened?"

"You fought the river. The river won." He skewered the animal—it looked to be a rabbit—and wedged the stick over the fire. He then turned another stick of meat that had already been cooking for some time. He pulled out his pipe, placed a small plug of weed mix in the bowl, and offered it to Berengial. Berengial shook his head, feeling a heavy, slow ache deep inside it and a sharper stinging pain just above his left eye. He reached up and felt a small cloth bandage on his forehead. How long had he been unconscious?

Tianati shrugged and lit his pipe. Berengial noticed the Little did not say his usual perfunctory prayer.

"You think we could drag that boat the rest of the way down the rapids?" Berengial asked. He had stopped worrying about showing weakness on this point. He would be damned if he'd go down that rushing death trap again.

"Sure. We're nearly at the bottom anyway."

Berengial saw Naamani stringing his clothes up to dry from low pine branches near the river. He realized he was unclothed under the blanket, and wondered whether Naamani had been the one to strip him down.

"How long 'til that rabbit's done?" Berengial said. He was suddenly very hungry. His stomach rumbled, a loud, low growl from deep inside his giant abdomen.

"Soon enough. Just wait," Tianati said.

Suddenly, from all around them, thousands of silent birds rose up at once, black and brown wings flashing and thrusting them into the sky above the trees, blurring the pines and the blocking the sun. Tianati made the mistake of looking up at the sight. While the Little was distracted, Berengial reached over and stole his rabbit.

"Dammit," said Tianati when he looked back again and found Berengial ravenously devouring the rabbit. "I should know better than to take my eyes off a giant."

Berengial saw Naamani looking over at him from under the pines with a barely-suppressed smile. He did not know why, but he thought she, at least, had not taken her eyes off him. And such eyes.

"Tianati saved your life," she said quietly but firmly, looking into his eyes without flinching. "The least you could do is thank him."

Berengial was surprised by her frankness. And also impressed. He turned to Tianati and made a half bow while seated, "My eternal thanks and gratitude, Tianati of the People." He turned back to Naamani. "Was that a good enough expression of gratitude to your master, Naamani?" He regretted his mocking tone as soon as he said it. But she didn't flinch.

"It was not Tianati who made me a slave, but it was he who saved your life."

Tianati watched the exchange unfold with interest, not saying anything. Berengial smiled. "I like your style, slave girl. So what's your story. Who did take your freedom?"

Naamani still did not take her eyes off him, but said nothing. Then she turned and silently hung up the rest of the wet clothes.

$$\text{☽ ● ☾}$$

Over the next several days they walked many miles, though their progress was slow, as they were carrying the longboat with them. At last they reached and passed the edges of the People's territory. The following night they stopped at a flat, dry place on a high bluff overlooking the river plain. A grove of ancient chestnut trees ringed a small clearing on the edge of the overhang. They had a clear view to the setting sun in the west. A cool breeze rustled the leaves as they sat around the fire munching on roasted chestnuts and more rabbit. Tianati looked into Naamani's eyes and saw a distant fire burning somewhere deep down. She startled him by looking right back into his eyes. "So you want to know how I came to be a slave?"

"Tell your story, Naamani. I wouldn't take a slave myself, and don't think anyone should. But my People did, and so I share in the blame. I deserve to know how I came to wrong you."

Naamani reached into her pouch and surprised him again by pulling out a plug of tobacco. She muttered a prayer in a foreign tongue and tossed the herb into the fire. "I come from the land far to the east, along the edge of the great eastern ocean. My family loves the sea and everything in it. We hunt the giant whales and seals and feast on oysters, clams, and lobster."

"Lobster?" asked Tianati.

"Like giant crawfish. They live at the bottom of the sea. They are delicious." Naamani took a breath and gathered herself. "Anyway, every summer we move up and down the coast following the animals of the sea, staying in sheltered villages in the winter. In the autumn two years ago, when I was seventeen years old, my six brothers and I prepared a summer's worth of seafood and provisions for the winter on a high dune over the beach. A company of your "People" came marching down the beach, singing some infernal song and pissing in the ocean. They took a fancy to me, and my brothers did not take kindly to their forwardness. First came the insults, then the fists, and then the knives. My brothers took down eight of your kind but all lost their lives. The two men left decided I would be compensation for their lost kin, and took me prisoner. They used me as they wished over the six months it took to travel over the mountains to your land. When they brought me to their town upriver from the big city, I killed them while they slept, cutting off their manhoods as a souvenir. That is how we handle such things in my family." She reached into her bag and pulled out a necklace dangling with two shriveled, dried genitalia. Tianati recoiled, and noticed that even the giant seemed shaken. "I knew the men's family would have me killed, so I went straight to your People's Council and told them the whole story. One of the councilwomen took pity on me and made me a slave of the Council. And now your slave." She stood and tossed another plug of tobacco into the fire, speaking in her native tongue again under her breath again. "Sleep well tonight," she said, as she turned to go to bed.

It was still dark when a warning hiss from the Allegh pulled Tianati from his sleep. "Tianati, get up. We have company." Tianati heard the dogs barking as the giant kicked him the ribs to make sure he awoke.

"Damn it, giant. Do you have to . . ." He stopped, and saw they were surrounded by forty strong armed men. He knew right away they were not of the People. They all wore elaborate beaded leather pants and headdresses of white eagle feathers. Tianati motioned to the giant to stay quiet, rose slowly and identified the men's captain, a tall older man with the most impressive headdress. Tianati did not know whether these warriors spoke the People's tongue. He decided to speak in the common tongue of trade.

"Greetings brave men. I am Tianati of the People, travelling peacefully with a message to my kin. With me are a friendly giant and a girl, Naamani."

The captain smiled. "You are fortunate to be traveling with a giant and a girl from the sea. If you had shown up here alone, a man of the People, you might not have made it out of this country alive. We are no friends of your 'People.'"

It was Tianati's turn to smile. "You're certainly not alone. Would you indulge my quick passage through your lands? I do not come to cause any problems."

"It is not our custom to ignore guests. You will either die here or feast with us. But our king must decide."

"King?" Tianati was surprised. He knew that the frontiers had many dissident clans. But he had not heard that any had named their own king. There had not been a king in these parts for centuries.

"Come with us," said the Captain, and the warriors formed a phalanx pointing north, with Tianati, the giant, and Naamani in the middle, leaving the longboat and provisions behind.

They marched under a dense hardwood canopy for several hours before emerging onto a bright, clear plateau ringed with low mounds shaped like turtles, bears, and eagles. A tall longhouse stood in the center of the complex, surrounded by forty or fifty smaller homes. The captain led them to a low platform adjacent to the longhouse, and told them to climb a small step-ladder up. They stood on the platform for what seemed like an hour, wondering at their fate, when a man, certain to be the king, emerged from the longhouse. He was short but powerfully built, gray-haired with a small wispy white beard, and no headdress at all. But he carried a scepter crowned with the beak and talons of an eagle that must have been amongst the largest of his kind. He looked at Tianati and burst out into loud song, an ancient ritual chant that startled Tianati. The words and meaning were archaic and strangely sung. Tianati barely understood their meaning, but gathered that it told of a time when all the tribes, clans and nations were one. With a fading final chorus, the eagle king stopped singing and began to speak.

"You who are called 'Tianati' know as well as I that the days of unity among us are gone forever. Your 'People' have lost the spirit. You take slaves again. You pray without meaning. You study the stars, moon and sun as if they were just numbers, instead of living beings full of spiritual energy. You are dead inside. We, the Nation of the Eagle, remember the old ways. We talk to the spirits of the land. But though we are living in truth and you are dead, you would overwhelm us with numbers, so we keep ourselves hidden. We live in the forests and glens, and it is rare that we let any of your kind live who gaze upon our villages. You have requested that we let you live and pass through our land unharmed. Before I pronounce your fate, I will grant you my ear. Tell me Tianati of the People, why should I let you live? You who would tell your people of our location and cause our destruction?"

Tianati took a deep breath and looked deeply into the king's eyes. "Brave King of the Nation of the Eagle, I come with respect and awe at your devotion to the old ways and spirits. I am a simple warrior, not a king, and will not pretend to understand the spirit world as you do. But there is one thing we share. Honor. I have never and will never break an oath. Today I give you my oath that if you let us pass through your land, I will never tell a soul you are here. And I will offer you something else.

If I ever have influence on the course our nation takes, I will advocate for your recognition as a free nation under your kingship."

The king laughed. "We need no 'recognition' from your soulless Council. When your cities are ruined and your people scattered, some of you will crawl to us for recognition. But I believe you are honest, warrior. I will accept your oath, and tomorrow one of our men will lead you back to your boat." He turned to his captain. "We shall feast tonight in honor of a giant, a slave, and their companion, who shall be our guests!" Tianati saw the giant smile at him, and thought he caught a wink.

The celebration was primeval, with drums and fire and dancing throughout the night. An old medicine man threw something pungent into the fire, and before too long Tianati's head was swirling from breathing it in. Finally he lay down away from the fire and closed his eyes. He couldn't sleep, but he wasn't awake either. Animals danced before his eyes. A bat, a wolf, thousands of small birds, a soaring eagle. His village priest would have told him these were his totems, his protective animal spirits. In the state he was in, Tianati would have believed it. Then the animals fled before a growing blue electrical storm. Swirling clouds of energy crackling with light and imbued with darkness filled Tianti's closed-eyed vision. At first he was afraid, pulling away from the storm. Then he relaxed, became the eagle, and flew higher and higher past bolts of hot white lightning, straight into the heart of the storm. The violence vanished and a white light blew like a gentle breeze on his face, which was a human face once more, caressing his cheek like a warm tongue. He opened his eyes to a bright morning with Naamani's dog Pug licking his face.

Later that morning, as they gathered their gear and readied to depart, the Eagle King approached Tianati. "Would you enter the steam lodge with me before you leave? I find that it makes the day after a festival better."

Tianati could not refuse the offer, though he rarely used a steam lodge. "I'd be honored." He followed the old king down a trail about a mile to a small cave-like hut covered in animal skins. The lodge keeper held open the east-facing flap, smudged each of them with cedar, and motioned for them to enter. Inside, they crawled to the south wall and sat as the lodge keeper entered and secured the flap. They made offerings of tobacco and said a prayer, and the lodge keeper placed the hot stones in the fire pit at the center of the lodge. After more prayers, he poured water over the hot stones, filling the small lodge with steam. He threw cedar and grasses into the fire as well, releasing pungent aromas. Tianati, the king, and the lodge keeper sat in the lodge for over an hour, no one saying a word, until the king turned to Tianati.

"This is a breach of tradition, but I want to talk with you in here, under the eye of the spirits."

Tianati had some difficulty focusing on the king's words. The steam, smoke, and heat had exhausted him, but he refused to show weakness. "What do you want to talk about?"

"I have no love lost for your People, but you I like. The Allegh who is traveling with you, I sense he conceals some dark truth from you. How did the war end?"

Tianati struggled to form his words, but managed to explain the war's end. He felt he had to justify his trust of the giant. "Giants hate and fear us, I believe, but they want a truce as much as we do. And it would not benefit this giant to harm me in any way. Our mission is for the benefit of his folk as well as mine."

"My spirit guides tell me otherwise, but you must follow your own. Now, open your mind's eye and try to see them."

Despite his skepticism, Tianati tried to see spirits, and perhaps because of the heat, smoke, and dehydration, he thought he glimpsed shapes moving up and down before him, wispy shapes vaguely resembling people, perhaps. But then the shapes vanished, and Tianati realized he had to get out of the tent. He managed to choke out a few words first. "Thank you king. Would you permit me to leave?" At the last word he stumbled through the flap, the lodge keeper opening it just in time. He fell on the ground outside, gasping the cool, clean air deeply.

The king came through the flap a moment later and laughed. "Come with me. Now comes the best part!" He pulled Tianati to his feet and led him a short distance away to a deep, cold, stone-ringed pond. Grabbing Tianati around the middle, he pulled him into the bracing waters.

Tianati's eyes flew open and he screamed. He bounded back out of the pond, shivering. The king stayed in the water, laughing as Tianati stalked back down the path towards the camp.

"Now you should be ready for the road!" the king called after him.

EIGHT

A STORY FOR SAK

The river was easy for some time after they left the Eagle King's town: the current steady and strong, the surface smooth and barely ruffled. They paddled even at night, taking turns sleeping to make time. Naamani hardly spoke at all. Tianati had long stretches when he could imagine he was alone in his own canoe again. The only sounds were the cries of a distant wildcat, the insistent hoot of a horned owl, and the liquid drip of his paddle in the moonlit water. He let his body do the work of guiding the longboat through the hard dimensions of space as his mind drifted freely through time.

He settled quickly into a pleasant memory—eleven years ago, when he was on his Mission. He had stopped in the principal town of the Mandan, just up from the split-trunk of the river, to rest for the night before continuing the difficult paddle up the Mississippi and its west fork towards the obsidian mines in the Great Rocky Mountains. At his naming ceremony, the Astronomer had assigned him the path of the black rock—the hard trek west to trade for as much of the obsidian as he could carry. The trip was more arduous than he had imagined. He had always prided himself on being the toughest traveler in his town. Though his frame was small, he packed tight muscles, and thought by sheer will he could paddle longer and jog quicker than the rest. This trip had taken a toll on him, however, and had tested his young pride.

The day he had arrived in the Mandan town, he'd pushed himself particularly hard. The rain had not stopped and the river was high. The water pushed up at him from the river and down on him from the sky. He felt like a little boy being held down by older boys. Not for the first time, he caught himself cursing the river and the rain. At last he saw a stone tower rising from the river that marked the location of the Mandan town.

He looked like a drowned squirrel when he showed up at the first house at the edge of town. His map beads suggested that when visiting the Mandan, it was polite to stop at the smallest house closest to the road and announce yourself to whoever lived there. From there, you would be escorted to a guesthouse selected by the King's wife. The Mandan knew at least some of his language, as did most people in the world, and were accustomed to his people travelling through. His gifts of pipe leaf and carved toys would be welcome. He would be expected to sing at least one new song and teach their bard the tune. Tianati hoped he would be allowed to sleep first. He did not even have an interest in a visit from their maidens, he was so exhausted.

When he announced himself politely at the smallest house closest to the road, he was greeted by a woman unlike any he had ever seen or heard of. Her hair was the color of late summer rye in the afternoon. Her eyes were ghost-like, light brown like white pine bark. Her skin was cinnamon hued, not much lighter than his own but less the color of earth than of wood. He could smell her too — a scent of mulberry wood and sun, even in the rain. She was young, but older than he, and taller. Her name was Lenai.

"Welcome little one," Lenai laughed, "why get wetter? Come in!" He had never even made it to the chief's house.

A change in the current forced his attention back to the present. After a few minutes of hard paddling to get the longboat back on course, Tianati wondered what Lenai looked like now, over a decade later. Tianati was startled to see the giant looking at him with a bemused smile. "I thought you were sleeping."

"Why don't we go see her?" asked the giant.

"Who?"

"The girl you've been fantasizing about since we passed the falls. You're not hard to read. Who is she, anyway?"

"Just a light-eyed kid I met a very long time ago. She's probably old and fat now, with ten little kids running around her thick ankles."

"Nice. With that kind of charm, I can't believe she didn't fall for you back then. Where's she live?"

"I have no idea. She was a Mandan and lived in a small town near a rock tower just up the Mississippi, the big river that joins the Ohio downriver from here. But that was so long ago she can't still be there. I wouldn't be surprised if the town had already moved."

"Can't hurt to try. We need to get some new spear and dart points before we head down the Mississippi anyway, right? Surely they'll have some spare flint at this Mandan town of yours. Let's go see your girlfriend."

"She won't be there." Tianati paddled for another hour without speaking. He watched the clouds that had brought the morning rains slowly break and clear, leaving sun and blue sky to brighten their way. "But I do need dart points," he said at last.

The giant paddled silently for a time. "Do you even remember her name?" he said at last.

"Lenai. Lenai of the Mandan. But she won't be there." Tianati hated to pray for himself. It made him feel small and weak. But he prayed he was wrong.

OOO

Berengial looked across the lake-like expanse of water where the Ohio became the Mississippi and wondered at how much rain must fall to make such a watercourse. At the point between the confluence of the rivers there was a marker of stone covered in strange symbols, surrounded by offerings of beads and flowers. Tianati steered the longboat to a sandy landing near the stone and climbed out. Naamani and her dogs sprang from the boat, happy for a chance to stretch and run. Tianati paused to take a smoke and leave a gift, offering a puff to Berengial. The giant took it, and didn't even cough. He had taken at least one puff a day since his headache faded after the falls. He preferred Tianati's sweet mix, the one with more hemp and cedar, a touch of mint, and less tobacco. It no longer made him dizzy. But it did make him talkative.

"I've never seen a Mandan girl before. You never told me, how was she built up top?"

Tianati glared at him. "Just right. Maybe you should try my bitter mix. This sweet one loosens your tongue too much."

☽ ● ☾

They set off up the Mississippi. This time, the weather was perfect. The river was low and slow. The trip that had taken Tianati a whole week of hard work on his Mission took just a few days now. He saw the mysterious tower in the river first, and knew they were close. The Mandan's town was still there.

"This it?"

"Yes, this is it. We have to announce ourselves at the smallest house closest to the road."

They parked the longboat on the boat ramp and walked up the road to town. The house where Tianati had met Lenai was not there. But there were many more houses—the town had grown. The homes were like artificial hills, large, circular mounds of earth with living space underneath and platforms on top.

Naamani looked around in wonder. "This looks like a nice place to live," she said, surprising Tianati and the giant, who were used to her silence. "Do they speak the People's tongue?"

Tianati looked at Naamani. "They do, and it's a friendly place. The Mandan are a very civil people. They eschew war and welcome visitors. But we must watch our manners." They stopped at what looked to be the smallest home closest to the road and politely announced themselves. A lanky old man came out and laughed. "You're a big one!" he said, eyeing up the giant. He hardly looked a Tianati. "Come in, King Moose," he said to the giant, smiling.

His house was small but well appointed. There were good pipes on a shelf and bags of smokeweed hanging. Several logs of even size served as chairs around a well-constructed fire pit. Tianati and the Giant sat on logs. Naamani sat on the floor a little ways back from the circle, her dogs curled around her. Tianati offered the old man a small bag of his good mix. The man gladly accepted, and in turn opened it to share.

They smoked silently before the old man spoke. "You look familiar. You've been to our town before." It wasn't a question. "Things have changed here. We've had many more visitors from South. Some I do not trust. Your people, we've always liked. You sing, you tell stories, you go easy on the girls. You bring the best smokeweed. The best toys. These folk from the South, they've come from far away. They seem to like to talk only of death. Their stories are all of war. All they eat is corn. Corn corn corn. I like a good corn fritter as much as the next man, but these folk want only corn. They care only for the sun. They mock the moon. They are rough to women. But they cannot be kept away. They don't take a hint."

Tianati searched his memory and found what he was looking for. "Sakshu, that's your friend-name, am I right?"

"You remember well. And you go by Tianati with friends, am I right, wise young one?"

"Yes, you can call me Tianati, though I fear I'm neither young nor wise."

"My real friends call my Sak. You I will call a real friend."

Tianati felt warmed by the old man's words and the cozy earthen hut. He wanted to bring the giant into the fold. "This is a giant, but a good man, and now my friend." Tianati realized as he said the words that they were true. He had become friends with a giant.

The giant smiled, bowed his big head, and formally greeted Sak. "Sakshu, my Little friends call me the giant, and I will share with you that my friend Tianati, though not a giant, is still a good man." Sak laughed so hard at the formal way the giant said "Little" that he bent over and nearly fell off his log. The giant and Tianati laughed too, though as much at Sak's convulsions as anything else.

When Sak finally stopped laughing, Tianati turned to Naamani, who he saw had fallen asleep between her dogs. "And this quiet one is Naamani. Our Council called her a slave, though she has helped us like a warrior."

All traces of laughter dropped from Sak's face. "I thought the People frowned on dealing in slaves."

Tianati sighed. "Like many things, that too is changing. Unfortunately, slavery has come back into fashion in many quarters of our land. For my part, I will never hold one, and when I finish this mission I hope to find a home where Naamani can be a free woman."

Sak looked at Tianati for a long time without speaking. Finally he nodded and said, "She would be welcome here. We can always use beautiful warriors." Sak paused and smoked. Tianati caught the giant looking at Naamani as she slept with an appraising eye. He too saw the girl for the first time as a striking young woman. *She is beautiful,* he thought.

Sak coughed, as if to draw their attention back to him. "Can you tell me how your people fare, and what became of the war between your people and the giants? If this causes strain with you two friends, please stay silent. But the tales and bits of stories that have come to us from that dark time have not been full. I've only heard a sliver of the moon. Give me the full moon, if you can."

Tianati thought for a while. He looked at the giant. The giant spoke first. "I think we can tell it best together. I will start by telling a part of the tale that Tianati has never heard." Tianati looked at him curiously. He had never heard of any giant telling a story. They were supposed to sing their tales. But the giant started in, in his own way. "We Allegh are a tall people. Hills are less of a burden to us. We like steepness. We like heights. Though our legends say we came from the land far to the south long, long ago, we found our true home in the hills and steep vales near the river that bears our name. We learned to befriend the fierce cats that haunt that land. They became to us as the dogs are to Tianati's folk. They slept within the light of our fires at night. We never sleep under a roof if we can help it. We think it a sign of weakness. But the cats came to sleep among us, never harming us, nor us them. They helped us hunt. They protected us from enemies. Our land became a place avoided by all other people. They called us the nation of cats. They thought that we and the cats were one—that we could change to puma form and back to human at will." The giant laughed. "We did nothing to quash the rumor. It kept us safe and happy in our hills. No one bothered us. We had the most beautiful country in the world to ourselves. We are simple. We like to hunt deer and wrestle bear. We hate to farm; even our women prefer to hunt. We love games. We hate to swim, but love to fish. All was good in our land. The 'Nation of the Cats.'" The giant laughed again, but this time with a little bitterness. "Then the city folk came." He tried to laugh again as he looked at Tianati, but it did not come out as a laugh.

Tianati thought it was time for him to take over the thread. "We've lived in the great rolling land of streams that lead to the Ohio for centuries, ever since our ancestors struck out from Zialand. You know our ways. All of our children travel when they come of age and receive their true name. On these travels we take our songs and our tales and our smokeweed, and we must return with something our Astronomer tells us to get. I had to bring back obsidian from the great western mountains. My sister was sent to the eastern coast for shells. Many are sent to bring back new blood—folks as different and interesting as can be found. We have had that tradition as long as anyone can remember. For a long time our rich land was more than enough of a mother to provide for all of us and more. Our numbers kept increasing, giving us strength, but our bounty made us the target for raids by the hungry tribes of the hinterlands.

"Eleven Nasakysus ago, about 209 years ago as you would reckon, some of us began to bring back giants from our travels. Many of the giants stayed among us, becoming part of the People, and raised families in the rich land we had built. They fought in our armies against the raiders, they lent their strength to the building of our roads and cities, and they could sing the low notes like no one else." He smiled at the giant, who did not smile back. "They also helped us keep peace with their cousins who lived in the hilly lands surrounding the Allegh's river. All was good in our land. But as our numbers increased, we needed to burn more land." Tianati looked again at the giant. "I should explain how we use fire."

"Yes, you should," said the giant, gravely.

Tianati explained the People's method of clearing the land by fire so that the plants and animals that sustained the people could prosper. He sighed. "But when we began to outgrow our home land, and move east and north, we came to lands where we had not yet burned. While many giants had come into our land, many more stayed in their own. But they lived on their land without making footprints, and our people slowly moved in, thinking it vacant, wild; as we pushed in we cleared the streams and widened the paths. We began to plant beans and squash. We cultivated the berries. We burned our fires. We didn't know we were causing harm to the giants. At least not at first."

The giant could not keep silent any longer. "Bearscat," he spat. "The Littles who first came onto our country knew we were there. They took our best clearings. They burned us out of our homes." The giant paused. "Sakshu, could I offer you a smoke?" He reached into Tianati's bag and pulled a plug, placed it in his own pipe and handed it to Sak. Sak took a pull and handed it back the giant. The giant took a deep pull on the pipe. Held it. Breathed out. And took one more. He sat for a long while without talking. No one else spoke either. Then the giant started again.

"My great grandfather told me the story of the first fires. But I didn't need stories. By the time I was seven I saw the smoke two hills from my house. After the woods burned, the Littles — they call themselves the "People" — came. At first, only a few, two or four at time. But then villages appeared on land that used to be wild hunting grounds for us and our cats. And they stayed. They planted in the ground, took our deer, our elk, our bison, our fish. Then one of their damned fires burned fifty-two women, children, and men to death as they celebrated a wedding. I knew some of them. Finally, we had been pushed far enough. Thousands of us gathered at a council at the springs we call holy, though we hate big crowds. We also hate war, but we were strong, and we were angry. So war we discussed. Our kin who had joined with the fire-burners in their fancy cities came to us, to try to talk us out of doing what we had to do. They said we should keep the peace. We should join the "People," we should suck on their smoke, swallow it. But our cousins had lost their spirit, their pride, and they seemed shameful and neutered. Hell, they even looked shorter to us. We sent them back to deliver a message that the Nation of the Cat was not to be taken without a fight. So we made war. We armored our pumas, sharpened our spears, and painted our faces. And we struck ten of the new Little villages in our land on one night, wiping them out."

He went silent, eyes closed, almost as if he relished the thought. Tianati looked at the side of his face, and spoke softly. "Too many were killed for the People to ignore the attack. We readied for war—the first real war we had fought in over a century. We were soft, truth be told. Soft and unprepared for the ferociousness of the giants. Whatever else giants are, they are vicious in battle." Tianati still looked at the giant's face; the Allegh's eyes stayed closed. "So we learned to become ruthless as well. The giants among us refused to fight. Most became so disheartened they left, and many of our own people left as well, in solidarity with the giants and against the war. They traveled back to our common ancestral homeland to the south, in the heart of Zialand.

"We took heavy losses in the early days of the war. But there were still many more of us than there were giants. The Astronomers, always good at numbers, figured out pretty quickly that we could lose more warriors than the Allegh did in each battle and still win the war. And in the early years, that is just what happened. The giants killed two or three of the People for every warrior they lost. But the math started to overwhelm them."

"Not just the math," the giant interrupted. "You learned to fight well, too." He spoke with the grudging respect of a warrior for a warrior. "They killed the big cats first, knowing how that stole our spirit. And they kept up that infernal burning, only this time not to clear weeds but to destroy our land, drive the deer away, keep us on the run. We knew it was over years before the war ended, but the stubborn among us shamed the wiser into continuing the fight long after we knew it could not be won."

It was Tianati's turn to interrupt. "But it was then that the giants pulled off a masterstroke. A small but hardened group of giant warriors, including the giant sitting here"—Tianati nodded at the giant with a great deal of respect—"penetrated to the heart of our land, to the central circle at the Great Observatory itself, and took control of our most sacred of places. There they could have killed our Astronomers, defiled our holy monuments, destroyed our carefully-built calendars and star trackers. But they didn't. They came to talk—not to surrender, but to talk from a position of strength. They came to end the war on terms that they could live with."

"We lost the war, but we won the peace." The giant seemed unable to disguise his pride. "We kept all the lands feeding our river, except for a few villages that the People had established, which were allowed to continue living under their rules but with our consent. We bet that the Littles were as tired of war as we were, despite their victories."

"My village, where I was born and raised, is in giant-country," Tianati said, "but until this trip, I had hardly exchanged ten words with a giant, even though our Astronomers urged us to increase contact. While both sides believe the peace is too important to let misunderstandings destroy it, the fear and distrust run deep." Tianati stopped. Not once in the thousand miles they had come together had they ever spoken about the war, at least not outside of a joke or two.

Sak took a deep drag of his pipe. He held the smoke inside his lungs for a long time, then let it creep out his nostrils. "I'm glad you city-folk and cat people worked out your little feud." He looked long and hard at the giant. "If indeed you really have."

$$\newline \mathcal{D}\bullet\mathcal{C}$$

The next morning, while Naamani was out gathering breakfast, Tianati asked Sak about Lenai. The old man's face saddened. "She was the light of our village. Voice like a songbird. Hair like wheat."

"Was? Did she marry and go to another village?"

"She never married. Ten years ago we lost her to a difficult childbirth. Her son has turned into the village trickster."

"Her son?" Tianati's mouth was suddenly dry.

"She named him as she lay dying. A strange name, though with some power."

"What's his name, Sak?"

"Rainseed. And Tianati, don't bother looking for him now. He's away for the summer in the mountains. He goes there every year. He says that's where his father went when he left his mother."

OOO

Berengial spent the day gathering and shaping flint at the quarry carved into the bluff above town. He was troubled at how hard it had been to lie to the Littles about the war and he was worried that the old man Sakshu had seen right through his deception.

"Breakfast, big one!" called Naamani from down in the village. Berengial gathered his finished spear points and dart heads, returned the unused flint to a basket left at the quarry for that purpose, and started down the hill.

I've got to be more careful, he thought to himself.

NINE

MOUTH CITY

They stayed in the Mandan's town long enough to stock up on flint, dried meat and corn, and necessary tools. Tianati saw that Naamani was sad when it came time to load the longboats and leave town. "Like this place?" he asked.

"I see no slaves here. Except for me, of course." She sounded bitter.

"Help us live through this thing and you can come back here, or wherever you want, as a free woman. I wish I could free you now, but the Council in its wisdom forbade it." He was planning on returning to the Mandan town himself anyway to meet Rainseed, who he thought might well be his son.

"Council," she spat. "Some wisdom. A wise people would've freed me and escorted me to the sea with a basket of valuable goods as restitution."

"I don't agree with everything they do, but when they issue a command, I'm bound to follow it." But even as he spoke the words, he thought they sounded cowardly and weak. Naamani said nothing more. She quietly fed and watered the dogs and loaded her satchel onto the longboat.

The weather stayed favorable, so they continued to travel by both day and night; the giant was happy to sleep through the day and paddle at night. Naamani had a knack for starting small cooking fires on a makeshift platform in the center of the boat, and her cooking was excellent. They ate fresh fish, turtle and duck, and snacked on dried fruit and corn. Someone was usually sleeping, so they rarely spoke. No one seemed unhappy with the quiet. They passed many villages and towns, but all were friendly to the People, and no one harassed them—though the farther downriver they went, the more stares the giant garnered. Tianati watched the changing scenery with great interest. He had never been this far south before. Large cypress swamps began to appear, the great knobby-kneed trees whispering of mysterious dark places inhospitable to men, women, and dogs.

It was early in the morning, just after he took over paddling duties from the giant, that Tianati saw his first gator. He had of course heard many stories of the great beasts, but the tales had not prepared him for the menacing power of the twelve-foot-long, scaly, toothed lizard that glared at him, jaws agape, from a sandy swath beneath a spreading cypress on the right bank. Naamani saw it too, and her eyes grew wide. Tianati quickly noticed there were twenty or thirty more lounging in and out of the water. The river was alive with gators.

Tianati remembered seeing something about the creatures in his bead map. "Keep us in the middle of the stream, Naamani," he said, handing a paddle to her. He ran his fingers through the map and its instructions until he found it. *Avoid swimming and fishing near gators, but they are good meat.* He laughed. The Council had a knack for the obvious. "Keep the fishing rods in the boat until we can't see the things," he whispered, though the gators seemed unconcerned with their boat. "Hopefully the giant won't tip our boat near these guys!"

Naamani smiled. "I think even those beasts might choke on that big meal."

By the time the giant awoke in the afternoon to the aroma of dinner cooking, they'd passed any sign of gators and had caught ten fat frogs.

OOO

Berengial woke hungry, as always. He was not usually a fan of frog, but Naamani had soaked the frogs in a brew of spices and fruit juices for several hours before grilling them, and the smell was making Berengial's mouth water. *I like this Little*, he thought.

"You missed the gators, giant." Tianati was already munching on the first round of grilled frog. "Better not tip this boat again. Even you would have your hands full with those monsters."

"Gators? We used to trade for dried gator meat with a band of travelers from the Petee coast. I love gator meat. Wake me the next time you see one."

"We've already seen a few hundred; I doubt you'll have to wait until tomorrow to get a shot."

Tianati was right. Berengial saw his first gator while still eating—a big one, floating lazily alongside their boat as if waiting for scraps. Berengial tossed a piece of grilled frog leg just in front of his big snout. The gator chomped the bite in a burst of speed that surprised even the giant, who was used to taming quick pumas. Berengial didn't miss a beat. He pulled out his long spear, stood carefully with one foot braced on the bow, and launched the spear into the gator's exposed back. The spear was strong, its point sharp and true, and the throw hard and straight. But the gator did not succumb. Instead, he dove and rolled with thrashing speed under water, emerging with the spear broken, its point still embedded in his dark green armor. Then, with three strong thrusts of his tail, he reached the boat and grabbed the side with his impossibly large and numerous teeth.

Naamani was closest, but she proved herself more than just a good cook. She poked the long frog skewer right in the gator's eye, causing him to release the boat just before it would have capsized. Despite the danger, Berengial found himself smiling fondly at Naamani. "Nice one!" he said.

He suddenly felt an overwhelming desire to show off. He pulled his long blade from its holster, grinned at Naamani, put the knife in his teeth, and leapt into the water after the injured gator. The beast had gone deep, and Berengial had to grasp about in the murky water for several anxious moments before he felt the scaly, thrashing tail whipping desperately. With his other hand he grabbed the tail from below and pulled hard. He wedged the tail under his right armpit, quickly grabbed the knife handle, and stabbed up into the gator's underbelly, pulling back quickly to rip open the tough hide. Then he had to let go and swim up for air. After gasping a deep breath he dove back down for the gator, finding him still thrashing at the bottom of the river. He pulled the beast with great difficulty to the knee of a cypress, and hauled himself out to sit in triumph on the knotty root. He flashed Naamani a big smile. But she did not smile back. Her scowl was equal parts disapproval and worry. Tianati, on the other hand, was hooting with complete appreciation.

"Roast gator for dinner!" he howled, clapping his hands in approval. "Looks like he got his licks in, giant." He pointed at Berengial's shoulder. In his excitement, Berengial had not even felt the bite, but somehow the gator had taken a chunk of flesh from his right shoulder, and the blood flowed freely.

Naamani blanched and turned her back. "Cook it yourselves, morons," she murmured.

Berengial's smile faded as he pulled the dying gator out of the water. Tianati paddled the boat over to help. "Don't worry about giants, Naamani, their hide is tougher than a gator's, and they wear bite scars like jewelry." He reached into his kit and pulled out a small cloth bag. "Hold this on the wound, giant. You'll get your scar faster and with less pain." He tossed the bag to Berengial, who pressed it into the wound. The bag smelled bitter and pungent, and burned like hell. But he kept it pressed against the bite.

"Naamani, don't worry," Berengial said. "I know how to cook gator meat just fine. Would you at least do me the honor of tasting my cooking?"

Naamani didn't turn around or speak. But Berengial could see her nod almost imperceptibly. That was enough for him.

)●(

They camped in a grove of pawpaw trees on a hillside near the river for four days while they processed the gator, feasting on gator and pawpaw fruit while curing the gator's hide and working the teeth into an assortment of jewelry and tools. Tianati made himself a new toolkit and belt from the cured hide. The giant made a necklace for Naamani from the teeth, which she stubbornly refused to wear.

True to his word, the giant also knew how to cook gator meat. He made a grill of soaked sticks and cooked the meat fast over a hot fire, sprinkling some cooking spices he'd managed to conceal from everyone else the whole trip over top. They smoked large quantities of meat and dried much of the fruit for their travels. When they were done, Tianati led them in a prayer of thanks to the gator's spirit. It was his first heartfelt prayer in some time. Berengial touched his wound with a gesture of admiration at the gator's tough fight. They continued downriver with their bodies, bags, and spirits replenished, and by the next morning Naamani was actually wearing her gator-tooth necklace, to the giant's obvious pleasure.

)●(

The river continued to widen and the number of villages and towns began to increase as they approached the infamous Mouth City. For generations, the People used tales of Mouth City to explain to children the dangers of rampant iniquity. "Going to Mouth City" had become a shorthand expression for moral depravity. Many of those accounts were exaggerated, pandering no doubt to what a story-teller's audience wanted to hear, but in Tianati's mind the city's name was synonymous with impiety and loose women. And he was very much looking forward to visiting it for the first time.

It was difficult to know when they came upon Mouth City proper. The frequency of towns increased until there was little distance between settlements, and people were everywhere on the banks and in the river. Pontoon piers jutted out into the wide river, and boats of every kind ferried folks and goods across and up and down the river. The air was thick with the savory smell of cooking fires.

What struck Tianati was the apparent lack of churches or temples of any kind. Every city and town in the land of the People had a church. Some were simple, small earthen rings with uneven sides, but most were respectable, near-perfect circles with well-tended walls and grounds, and a few were massive ceremonial centers capable of hosting thousands, such as the circle at the site of the Great Observatory. The absence of any kind of order or ceremony whatsoever seemed to be the defining characteristic of this sprawling, crawling mass of people living on the last reliably dry land before the Mississippi began its dance with the ocean.

"You sure you want to stay here?" asked the giant. He seemed uneasy with the masses of strangers.

"We have no choice," said Tianati. "We have to find someone to help us secure an ocean-going boat, and we need to recruit a navigator to help us cross the great sea. This is the only place we can do that. We're going to be here awhile."

"Great news. I hope they don't eat giants here."

Tianati smiled. He knew the Allegh did not like to call themselves "giants."

"Doubt it. The gators eat everything, though, and will want vengeance on you, so watch your step."

In truth, the weeks floating downstream from the pawpaw patch campsite had depleted their food stores and left all of them drained and in need of rest and sustenance, both of which could be had in abundance in Mouth City. Tianati imagined eating and sleeping, and perhaps lovemaking, were all the Mouth City denizens seemed to do, based on appearances.

"Let's go up that hill there," Tianati said, pointing to a slope about half a mile above the river where a group of neat wooden homes stood a little apart from the rest on a slight bluff. The houses bore all the signs of the homes of the People.

"Why, so I can be even more hated?"

Tianati looked at him curiously. "Why would these people dislike you any more than usual? They've been far away from our war."

The giant refused to answer. Tianati shrugged and started up the hillside. The giant stood and watched him, then sat down on a rock near the edge of the path and waited stubbornly. Naamani shook her head as if displeased with a child's behavior and walked up with Tianati.

OOO

Berengial did not like Mouth City. The crowds, smells, and heat all depressed him. To make matters worse, Berengial had been told a story in his childhood of a large group of the People who hated the Allegh. They tried to destroy the alliance between the People and the Allegh by waging a campaign of violence and terror against the Allegh, including Allegh children. Eventually, the rest of the People had exiled this antagonistic group from the Ohio valley. In the story Berengial heard, the group had travelled downriver to Mouth City, where they plotted their return to slaughter Allegh children. The People had largely forgotten the matter, but the Allegh had preserved the memory of the Allegh-haters in a song that was part of every child's education. The distrust Berengial had of Littles in general was nothing next to the hatred he had of Littles living in Mouth City. Still, he had to get to Zialand, and he would need the Littles to help him get there. And he realized he did not want to disappoint Naamani. Reluctantly, he got off the rock and followed Tianati up the hill to the People's homes.

)●(

Tianati stood outside the small house and saw the giant starting to follow him up the hill. He knocked on the door frame and called out a greeting.

The door opened and a short, slim man smiled. "Hallo traveler!" he said in a strange, lilting accent.

"Hallo native!" Tianati said, and smiled. "I've come from the north reaches via the People's City. I have stories to tell and smokeweed to share. Do you have room for us?"

"Of course of course! I only hope you can bear my meager home, and can abide a hard floor and old blanket."

"And I hope," Tianati said cautiously, "that you can also abide a giant."

The man laughed. "The jokes up north have changed since my naming; I have to admit I don't get the current humor. But you're welcome to stay, my friend."

Tianati looked at him and his smile faded. "Friend, I'm a messenger for the Chief Astronomer and People's Council. I carry their own copper tale, telling of the end of the great war. At their direction one of my companions is of the Allegh people. He is a giant. I do not joke. Can you still abide?" Tianati gestured down the hill to where the giant and Naamani loitered.

The man was clearly taken aback. He paused, as if considering his words before speaking. Finally, he said, "Who was named Chief Astronomer?"

"Benchag of Hairy Creek."

"And who won the Ball Games this year?"

"The damned Kan Tuks, again."

The man smiled. "Kan Tuks cheat." He paused. "This giant of yours, is he dangerous?"

"Are you?" Tianati asked.

The man grinned wider. "I like you. What's your traveling name?"

"Tianati. And yours?"

"Checko. Tianati, this giant is your responsibility. If he so much as looks at my family the wrong way I'm holding you responsible. Agreed?"

"Agreed. I'm thankful for your hospitality. We'll be here before sundown with some food for you. How many in your family?"

"Six. No need to bring anything. Except your stories. And your weed."

"See you tonight, Checko."

$$\text{☽ ● ☾}$$

Tianati and the giant scrounged some fresh alligator meat and Naamani gathered some vegetables and herbs. They bundled the food to take to Checko's house despite his protestations, and showed up at his doorstep before sundown. Tianati told the giant to hold the food while he called out a greeting. "Can't hurt," he said.

Checko welcomed them warmly into his small home, and gladly took the food. "This gator will go well with the paw paws. Have a seat; make yourselves at home. My family welcomes you. I will prepare our dinner." A short woman with thin, strong arms smiled shyly; behind her four small children stared at the giant with wonder and fear. Tianati introduced the giant and Naamani to Checko's family and sat cross-legged on the floor. Naamani joined Checko to help prepare dinner. When the food was ready, Checko placed large bowls before each of his guests, and smaller bowls before his wife and children. He smiled at the giant. "Have you ever been this far from home, big man?"

"No, little man," the giant said, without a smile. The two looked each over cautiously. Tianati stepped into the conversation.

"Have you had good rains this year, Checko?"

"We've had enough so far this season, but this week has been bone dry. And hot. Maybe your coming will bring rain." Checko paused, as if wondering what else their coming might bring. "Enough with the weather, tell me of the war's end."

"Are you here because of the war?" Tianati took a bite of the gator paw paw stew. It was delicious, with a spiciness unlike anything he'd tasted.

"Oh no. I came here on my Mission. The Chief Astronomer sent me south for conch shells and jade. I found Sherriancha," he pointed to his wiry little companion, who broke into a toothy grin, "and found I had no wish to go back to a land with snow and giants."

The giant glared but said nothing.

"Did you send word?" Tianati asked, "or are you one of the Missing?"

"I told a young girl on a Mission to tell the Chief I wasn't coming back, but that I would keep a small church here and would welcome travelers of the People, such as yourself. Yourselves," he corrected himself, glancing sideways at the giant.

Tianati took a breath. He had hoped the good food would dispel some of the fear and animosity between Checko and the giant, but he felt the tension in the room increasing, and dredging up the war was sure to inflame both of them further. "I hope you'll forgive me Checko, but I'm weary of talking war. My task — our task — requires us to travel across the sea to Zialand, and then inland to the City of Gods. We are staying here just long enough to find a boat and a guide to take us across the ocean." Tianati had finished his stew. He reached into his bag for some leaf. "Can I offer you some good People's smoke?"

Checko smiled broadly. "If the giant will smoke with me."

Tianati looked at the Allegh, who was still glowering silently. Tianati lit the pipe, took a puff slowly, and handed it to the giant. The giant took it, feigned a puff, and handed it grudgingly to Checko.

"Have to say," Checko said in between deep draws, "I've never smoked after a giant before. The weed tastes just as good, though!" He laughed. The giant did not. "It won't be so easy to find a navigator to help you cross the great sea now. The smart ones stay close to shore this time of year. The big storms can come up fast." He paused. "But I do know of one guy crazy enough to cross with you. You'd have to part with something nice, like a bag of your good leaf, and you'd have to put up with a cranky old sot, but he'd get you there."

"Much as I hate to part with it, I will pay if need be. Who is this character?"

The giant spoke for the first time in a while. "It is this character right here; can't you see where he's going with his word game? Tianati, we should stay off the water and hike. There has to be a path to Zialand."

Tianati started to answer but Checko interrupted. "You big oaf, you don't know the land south of here at all. Trackless desert lies to the interior, and the narrow coastal strip is haunted by cannibals, and worse. Why don't you let us civilized folk sort this out?"

Tianati could see where this was heading. He stood and put his hands on Checko's shoulders. "You will apologize to my friend the giant, and hold your tongue." He turned to the giant, who already had rose and taken a large step towards Checko. "Easy, giant. We have a job to do."

The giant looked as if he'd rip Checko's arms off, but he stayed still. "I'll be damned if I'll sit in a boat for a month with this clown!" He turned and stalked noisily from the small house without waiting for an apology.

Tianati looked after the departing Allegh and shook his head. "Don't worry, I'll bring him around. But you can't taunt him like that. How soon can we leave?"

"Give me a week to get the family ready. I know where you can get a boat as well."

"Here's your leaf." Tianati packed one of his small spare leather bags with a generous handful of the fragrant mix from home, and tossed it to Checko. "You get us there and back and the giant and I will help you expand your house and church."

Checko grinned again. "I'll get you to the coast of Zialand, but you'll have to find your own way to the City of the Gods and back. I can't be away from Sherriancha and the kids for as long as that will take."

"That will have to do. Now if you'll excuse me I've got a giant to calm. Naamani, can you tend to the dogs and start gathering provisions?"

"Sure, unless you want me to help you track down the giant."

"You stay here and help Checko. Leave the giant to me."

Tianati spent the rest of the evening searching for the giant in the winding narrow pathways of Mouth City, only to find him hours later stretched out asleep on a grassy bluff at the edge of town. Tianati lay down nearby and watched the stars. What motivates a giant? he thought.

Not good leaf. Not fancy beads. Can't offer good shoes—couldn't find ones big enough anyway. He looked at the constellation the People called Cold Northman's Wife. Then it came to him. Women. Giants love strange women. The war had generated many stereotypes of the giants, some true, some not. But one reputation they had earned well was a love of women from different peoples. The giant women were strong and wise, but few called them beautiful. Marriages between giant women and non-giant men were very rare. Giant men, however, were strangely attractive to women, and such affections were freely returned. A plan to induce the giant into a mood more conducive to traveling with Checko began to form just as Tianati started drifting off to sleep.

$$\mathbb{D} \bullet \mathbb{C}$$

Tianati was able to wake before the giant, and had two servings of left-over stew from Checko's hospitality heating over a fire when the giant began to rouse. Tianati handed him a steaming bowl and said "good morning!" just a little too cheerfully.

"How'd you find me?" the Allegh growled.

"Easy. I looked for the largest lump in town. Wake up, giant. I need your help today finding something."

"What, another bigoted old sailor to spend the next month with?"

"No, you big ass. Girls. It's been a long time for me. Too long. Come on, this town is supposed to be crawling with them."

Tianati's gambit worked. He and the giant spent the better part of the day stalking the places young women frequented. They found a sandy beach along the river in the early afternoon where no one seemed to be working at anything other than frolic and flirtation. For two hours they played a concocted game half in the water involving a ball and some baskets with two ladies who seemed alternately enthralled and terrified of the giant. As the sun began to die in the western sky they built a fire on the sand and roasted some corn and mussels. The giant soon paired off with the smaller and darker of the girls and disappeared behind a small bluff, leaving Tianati alone with her friend.

"I thought the giants were a myth," she said. Her accent was new to Tianati, with a strange lilt and rhythm Tianati found enchanting. She said her people had come from the great swamp that spanned the flat penisula well to the south and east. "My grandparents used to scare us kids with tales of huge flesh-eating ogres in the distant north, who would come down to the south to feed on children who misbehaved. Now I see they're real, but not at all what I feared."

"My people have spent the better part of the last decade warring with them. I can tell you they can be more ferocious than the worst childhood nightmare."

She rested her head against his shoulder. He pulled her closer and kissed the top of her head. Her soft hair smelled sweet, like honeysuckle. He lay back against the cool sand, pulling her on top of him. She looked in his eyes and slid her warm thighs on either side of his hips, running her hands slowly down the sides of his head. "Did your people win?"

Tianati looked at her from hair to belly while his hands followed along, stopping to hold her hips firmly, pushing her moistness against him. "My people never lose." His leather pants parted as he lifted her up just enough to let him slide into her.

"I can tell you don't lose," she sighed. She rocked back to let him slide in, and stayed leaning back while grinding up and down in a slow, excruciating variation on a dance. He let her lead while playing with her small, firm breasts, holding on to his rising tide as long as he could. She began to sing as she danced, a breathy, tuneless song with rising volume and ragged beat that soon became one long cry of pure need and then joy. He realized then, with some chagrin, that he had not even learned her name.

☽●☾

The girls were gone when Tianati woke to the smell of roasting ga-tor meat. The giant smiled at him from behind the fire. "I can see why you were such a good soldier, Tianati." The giant handed him a roasted meat stick. "You know how to execute a tactical maneuver."

Tianati laughed. "If we can't get laid in Mouth City, we can't get laid anywhere." He took a bite of the meat. It was tough, but the giant had spiced it with some of the local hot rub, and it had a nice burn. He looked at the giant. "Did you enjoy yourself?"

"We just talked. She had some interesting criticisms of your 'People.' Apparently your folk aren't very popular here in Mouth City. Presumptuous pricks, according to Kiana. I told her about Naamani. She was not surprised to learn that you deal in slaves."

"I hope you did more than chat with Kiana about politics."

"Just talk. Why?"

Tianati looked at him. Then it came to him. "You're falling for Naamani," he said. The giant stayed silent. Tianati poked the fire and grabbed another skewer. *This could be trouble*, he thought, *or an opportunity*. He realized that a love affair on the long sea journey could be a big-ger problem than the hostility between Checko and the giant, but he also thought he could use the situation to do some good. He kept his thoughts to himself and changed the topic. "I think that clown Checko is our only chance to get across the ocean alive. We both have our or-ders. Can't you suffer through his nonsense for a couple of weeks?"

The giant poked a stick in the fire, then threw it in. "Just don't blame me if I throw him to the fish."

"If either you or I could sail the ocean, I wouldn't care. Without him, we're both fish food."

☽●☾

The week Checko said he needed to find a boat turned into two and then three as he ran into some difficulties. The first lender had already rented his out. The second had only a vessel so unseaworthy Checko called it a wet grave. Finally, after nearly a month, Checko found a boat large enough and sound enough to cross the ocean, with a little luck.

Sailing day dawned bright, hot, and still. The marshes around Mouth City sent forth hordes of biting mosquitoes and flies and a putrid stench of old death. Tianati looked at the boat Checko had managed to procure. "That's going to make it across the ocean?"

"Maybe. Maybe not. It's all we've got." Checko spat and tossed a heavy bag of provisions onto the small vessel pulled up on the sandy bank of the river. Tianati had never seen a boat quite like it. It was a flat and square raft with a thin mast in the middle. Two boards were fitted in slots on the sides, and could be lowered down into the water. A long oar serving as the rudder ran from a forked mount off the back of the vessel. The raft was made of a light wood Tianati had never before encountered.

"This comes from Zialand," said Checko. "They call it a Balsaboat. Let's hope the storms stay far away." He loaded some fishing gear on the raft in a built-in box designed for that purpose. "Do you have enough food and water for two weeks in case the fish stay away?"

"I think we'll be fine. I have jerky, dried corn, and ten big canteens." Tianati started loading his gear on the raft. A small tent of leather in the middle of the craft served as the only shelter, and when he looked inside he found two built-in boxes for storing food and water. The giant filled one with the water while Tianati loaded the food in the other.

"Bring more water. The sea will dry us out faster than you think," said Checko.

Without speaking, the giant turned and ran up the hill towards town with great leaping bounds. Tianati knew he'd return soon with more water than any normal-sized man could carry in two trips. "On its way," he said to Checko. "Naamani, can you try to find a few more fishhooks?" She left for a supply hut nearby. With the giant and Naamani gone, Tianati moved closer to Checko. "You know we appreciate your help on this trip, but I think you should go easy on the giant. The last thing we need is a fight on the open ocean."

"Like I said before, that giant is your responsibility. Just keep him off me and we won't have any trouble."

"Easier to do if you keep your tongue in check, Checko. One more thing. Don't you think it's a bad idea to bring dogs on such a long sea voyage?"

"Not really."

"Checko," Tianati said, "let me ask you again, slowly. Don't you think the dogs and their master should stay behind?" Tianati gestured up the hill to where Naamani stared longingly after the giant. "Imagine having to listen to those two lovebirds for a month on a small boat," he whispered.

Checko's eyebrows went up in bemused understanding. "Ah, yes. Dogs are a really bad idea on a boat. Way too much . . . barking. I'll say something."

The giant came over the hill loaded with canteens. "Enough?" he called to Tianati.

"Should be fine, thanks."

"No problem. Let's hope this boat can hold all of it and us."

"Yeah, let's hope — like me, it's never had to host a giant before." Checko grinned. Tianati did not. "You know, we're going to have to leave the dogs here. Have you made arrangements?"

"What!" said Naamani, "we can't leave Pug and Huk behind! They've stood watch for us all the way from the People's City. If it weren't for them, you might have had your throats cut by those eagle warriors while you snored. I will not leave them behind."

"Those dogs have been great on the river boat," the giant said. "They haven't caused any problems at all, and believe me, I would have noticed. I hate dogs."

"That's not the problem, giant. The problem is they drink water. We'll be short on water as it is," said Checko.

Tianati looked at Naamani. "You don't need to abandon the dogs. I have a mission for you. Take the dogs and go to the Mandan's town. Once you are there, I deem you free." Tianati knew he was risking the Council's ire by freeing the girl, and knew that the excuse he'd come up with — a romance in tight quarters that could spark tempers — was flimsy. But he feared he might not have another chance to free her. And there was something else he wanted her to do. "Take this with you." He handed her a small bead string, made for a child. "I have a half-sister. Her name is Apeni. We share a father. Our father and both our mothers are all dead. I am the only close family she has left. She worries too much for me, and I for her. You will probably see some of the People heading north as you travel. When you do, please give them this bead story and tell them to take it Apeni, daughter of Freeghalia, of the Northeast Frontier, with the message that I am still alive.

Naamani looked at the bead string. "What does it say?" She could not read bead strings.

"It is just a child's story. One we shared growing up. She will take comfort in the message."

Naamani nodded, then threw her arms around Tianati and hugged him deeply. "Thank you," she whispered in his ear. Then she grabbed the giant's hand and led him far enough away that they could speak without being overheard. They stood huddled closely, speaking in low tones for some time, and then embraced. Naamani walked back, shouldered her pack, called the dogs, and left, tears streaming silently down her face.

Part III

Storms

Autumn, Year 472

All the world is human.

-Bartolome de Las Casas

A Short Account of the
Destruction of the Indies

TEN

JOKES FOR THE MANNATATTOS

Tianati had heard stories and songs of the ocean from the time he was a young child, but nothing had prepared him for the vastness and power of the open sea. It took but a day of travel under steady breezes for the coastline to become a thin grey blur on the distant horizon. The sky was a great, blue, cloudless dome. The salty air seemed to swell Tianati's lungs, and he found himself strangely invigorated. Porpoises paced beside their small boat like pack dogs around a sled. The giant seemed worried by their closeness, and held his paddle as if to fend them off.

"They're our friends," said Checko, "it's the sharks we need to worry about. Sharks hate porpoises. When the porpoises leave, that's when you start to worry." This did not seem to calm the giant one bit. In fact, everything about the ocean seemed to diminish him. He could not comfortably stand without tipping the boat. After only a few hours of sea travel, his skin turned a greenish pale, and he looked ready to vomit at the slightest provocation. He did not eat at all the first day, and only sipped at his canteen.

Tianati, on the other hand, felt he was growing on the sea. He felt more alive than he could ever remember feeling. Checko gave him more and more to do each day with the boat, until Tianati was handling most of the daily sailing chores. After the first day, his skin had turned red and was sore. But he remembered the copper tube the junior Astronomer had given him at the Council, and began rubbing the strange lotion on his face and shoulders, and made the giant use some too; after another day, the sun stopped bothering him. On the third day, Checko was sleeping under the lean-to and the giant was rolling fitfully below the sail when Tianati noticed the sea was no longer flat and calm, but instead had become choppy, like the big lake would get on windy days. The sky, too had changed, from a high, clear blue to a thin grey gruel.

"Checko, wake up," Tianti called. "Checko!"

"Keep it down, I'm sleeping here."

"Do we need to tie anything down better? Like the giant? It's getting rough."

Checko sat up and looked around. "This is nothing, at least, not yet. But we better wake up the giant. It's going to get worse before it gets better." He took over the steering and set a course for the distant land.

"This might be a good time to find a dry piece of land for a night or two," he muttered, looking nervously at the gathering gloom. Lightning could be seen on the horizon, and sheer curtains of water rising up to the sky began to march slowly towards the little raft. The choppy waves had started to turn into longer rolls and swells, and the raft began to tilt at an uncomfortable angle on either side of the sea's moving hills. They had not seen a porpoise for hours. Tianati roused the Allegh.

"How far are we from land?" hissed the giant through clenched teeth and green lips.

"Could be a few hours before we get to shore, could be never," Checko laughed. "Probably feel like forever to you either way. If we're lucky, we can ride some of the storm's winds towards land. Giant, I could use your strength. Hold this rope here and don't let it slip."

Though he grimaced, the Allegh seemed grateful to have something to occupy him. Tianati helped steer while Checko gauged the wind and tried to keep the shore within sight. It was becoming harder and harder for them to see. Rain started falling in large, cold drops, first vertically and then at a steeper and steeper angle, until the wind and the water blurred together in a freezing, stinging wall of hell. Twice Tianati thought he would be tossed off the raft by the swells. The giant actually fell half in the water; only his death grip on the rope Checko had assigned to him kept him from getting washed to sea. Checko and Tianati pulled him back onto his perch near the lean-to, Checko chuckling, Tianati grim, the giant silent but clearly shaken. The wind grew impossibly strong, driving water into their skin like thousands of small, cutting stones. They could see nothing. Without any warning at all, a wave hurled the raft into a dense stand of tangled mangroves. Tianati heard the sound of cracking planks and the bellow of the bewildered and exhausted giant. After a moment's pause, during which the lack of movement was as disorienting as anything they had just been through, Checko laughed.

"We're alive!" Checko reached down behind him and broke off a splintered piece of their raft. "Our boat didn't fare as well, though."

Tianati looked down. "Doesn't look like we're actually on land just yet." The mangroves grew in a shallow, murky wash, and the waves kept crashing in and out, traveling on through the grove without any sign of stopping. They could see only a few feet through the dense branches and driving rain; there was no way to know how far they were from dry land. But it was clear that the boat would no longer work.

"Grab what you want to keep from the boat, and as much water as you can carry," Checko yelled. "We need to start clawing though this scat and find a spot to camp." Checko grabbed two canteens, his pipe bag, and some jerky. "Come on, this storm isn't getting better."

Tianati and the giant grabbed what they could and followed Checko as he clambered slowly and painfully through the lower branches of the mangroves. They were climbing horizontally more than walking, and after three excruciating hours they were still in the thick of the grove, with no sign of land. A large wave crashed over them, smashing Tianati's head against a thin but hard mangrove branch. "Scat! Any idea when we'll get out of this stuff Checko?"

Checko was about twenty yards ahead. He didn't answer, just pointed at a slight break in the trees to his right. Tianati and the giant quickened their pace and headed for the break. A low mound of land covered in dwarf oak trees spread before them like an oasis. The wind was louder and stronger than ever, and the rain pelted their raw skin, but they could barely restrain their happiness at finding earth.

"Whoooo!" shouted the giant, as he threw himself down under the low branches of the largest oak. He lay there panting on his back, arms outstretched on the wet, muddy ground, rain drumming his giant smile. "No humping way I'm ever going on the sea again, I can tell you that right now."

"You'll have to," said Checko soberly, "unless you want to die here. This isn't really the land. We're on an island, probably several miles from the coast. Unless you care to swim with the sharks, you're going to have to get back in a boat. That is, if we can actually build a new seaworthy boat; it won't be easy in this forsaken place."

"Listen, you clown, we barely made it out alive, and I can still hardly hear myself scream in this storm. I'll float to shore on your dead body before I go back out on that ocean."

"Hey, we aren't going anywhere until this storm passes," said Tianati, "Let's settle down and try to get a little shelter for the night. I think I can get this tree down. Give me a hand, will you?" Tianati started chopping a smaller oak with his hatchet. The giant got up and grabbed the trunk high up, pulling it away from Tianati's chops, until they started to hear the tree crack and break. They brought down four trees that way, and started weaving the branches into a makeshift wall and roof against the wind and rain, working the smaller branches like ropes against the branches and trunks of two smaller trees they left standing. Checko built a low platform from fallen timbers and they built a serviceable floor on that to keep them a little above the mud. As night began to fall, they had built a shelter just big enough for the three of them to lie down in, with the giant in the middle. The giant and Checko were wedged against each other, which was not to either's liking, but the close proximity helped to slightly warm their drenched bodies. Exhausted, they fell into a deep sleep almost at once.

Tianati awoke to a muggy and hot day and an empty shelter, grasping at the remnants of a dream he could not quite remember. Sometime in the night the storm had blown over, and Tianati was surprised to see that the ocean was visible on three sides. Their oasis was a small, raised point of land with thin lines of mangroves to the north and west through which they could see open water, a narrow beach to the south, and the dense grove they had travelled through to the east and southeast. Checko and the giant had already started building a raft using the wall of the lean-to as a base.

"Hey Tianati, why don't you try to walk around the island and find the remains of our boat? If the giant and I can finish this raft we'll float it around to pick you up," Checko said.

Tianati was taken aback at the sudden familiarity and apparent teamwork between Checko and the giant. He had not seen them work together so well on anything before. "I'll see what I can find," he said, and headed off down the small beach and out into the shallow water. The bottom was sandy and smooth. He found it surprisingly easy to walk in the water, and rather enjoyed the scenery. To the south, another mangrove isle much like the one they were on was only a few hundred yards away, and to the west, he could see a line of trees that looked like land. The shallow salt water teemed with fish and crab, though none bothered Tianati as he made his way around the island. As he rounded the south end and started heading east, the walk became harder. Deep holes pocked the sea floor, forcing him to swim short stretches. Eventually, he found it easier just to swim, keeping the line of mangroves at a comfortable distance to his left. Every few minutes he stopped, paddled in place, and peered into the trees, looking for pieces of the boat. After a few hours, he climbed up onto a mangrove root to rest. Looking out into the ocean, he was startled to see a small raft floating a mile or so out. At first, he thought it was his own boat, but then he saw three figures moving on the raft.

He froze, in case they were unfriendly. He could see two of the figures pointing towards where he sat. He tried very hard not to move and to appear to be part of the tree. The wind was taking the raft past the island, but he saw the sail drop and the paddles come out. The raft started coming slowly in his direction. Tianati had to decide whether to hide or make himself known. He carefully looked around for a place to hide, and saw over his left shoulder a flapping brown flag on the top of a mangrove fifty feet away. No, it was no flag, it was the remains of their old boat's sail, caught in the high branches of the tree. That must have been what the men on the raft saw, he thought.

He slowly moved deeper into the mangroves, finding a spot between two thicker trunks to hide. He sat still, moving only to munch some jerky. From where he was perched, he could see the raft making its way towards the island. He began to see the faces of the three men paddling the raft. They wore their hair long and loose around their shoulders, and looked young, almost boys. They carried rods and long spears. Fishing, thought Tianati. Just fishing. He felt sure that if worse came to worst he could kill them. But he did not want to kill them. He wanted to use their boat and find their village. Judging by the lack of provisions on the raft, they could not be very far from home.

As the young men closed in on the mangroves, Tianati started to make out their words. Though he did not know their language, it sounded close enough to trade speech that he felt sure he could make himself understood. He climbed out from his hiding spot and called out in a loud voice the common greeting in the trade tongue: "Hallo, friends and traders!"

The young men stopped paddling. The biggest one reached down and pulled out an atlatl, loading a dart and staring intently at Tianati. "Who are you?" one of the men called out in the common tongue of trade.

Tianati held up his hand in a gesture of peace and welcome. "Tianati of the People. My companions and I were tossed up on this island by yesterday's storm. We can trade stories, songs, news, and to-bacco for a ride on your boat and a few days in your town."

"Where are your friends?"

"On the other side of the island, trying to build a raft. I suspect they're not having much success."

The shortest of the three laughed. "Mangrove wood makes terrible boats."

Tianati smiled. "Think we can ride with you?"

"Sure. But you'll have to talk to our chief when you get to town. He'll want to make sure you're not spies from Mouth City."

"We just came from there, but our only allegiance is to the People far to the north, up the great river."

"Tell it to the chief," said the big one, "and I want a damn good story on the ride to town." The young man who had yet to speak rolled his eyes at his friend's bluster.

"You have a deal. Can I ask your names?"

"I'm Hakkida," said the big one, "of the Mannatattos."

"Gensoarato," said the smallest one.

"Fisherbird," said the quiet one. "Now of the Mannatattos, born of the Sea Peoples, who you may know as the Karankawas." He looked hard at Tianati, his face betraying nothing, his words flat, but Tianati was sure the boy was trying to tell him something else. *I am being warned,* he thought.

☽ ● ☾

Tianati saw Checko and the giant floundering just off the beach with an ugly and half-sunken raft as the Mannatattos paddled their craft around the end of the island. "Ho, guys, I found us a better ride!"

Checko looked up with a start. The giant looked as if he would reach for a weapon.

"Easy big guy, these are friends. For a song and a smoke, they'll take us to their village."

"We'll be fine, thanks, with our own raft," said Checko.

Tianati laughed. The raft actually sank further as Checko spoke. "Just get your stuff and climb on."

Fisherbird looked at the giant and smiled. "An Allegh. I thought your people were just a story told to scare children!"

Checko looked sideways at Fisherbird. "You a Karankawa? I heard your kind eat people."

Fisherbird blanched. "Lies. We are no cannibals."

Hakkida interrupted, looking at Tianati. "You said nothing of a giant. Is he tame?"

The giant growled. "Not to assholes."

"Easy folks," said Tianati. "He's an ally of my people, on a mission with me to deliver a message. Tame is not the right word, but he'll do no harm unless provoked."

Hakkida looked skeptical, but Fisherbird said, "The chief will want to talk with a real giant, Hakkida, you know that. You'll be praised for bringing such a novelty to his house!"

Tianati watched Fisherbird as he spoke. *This one is not what he seems.* But the Mannatattos were their best hope, maybe only hope, of surviving and getting back on their way.

"And you have not had smokeweed such as I bring, I promise that too!" Tianati said.

☽●☾

Before night fell the Manatattos paddled the raft up on a sandy beach on the mainland. They camped for the night on the beach, eating crabs and grouper and smoking some of Tianati's tobacco mix. Tianati let Checko and Gensoarato trade tall tales and stories, while he watched Fisherbird.

"One time, I was paddling up this creek, hunting gator, when I stumbled on a gang of cannibals," Checko said. "These humpers thought they had dinner floating right up the river to them. Three of 'em." Checko stopped and took a draw of Tianati's dream mix. He'd been talked into breaking it out, against his better judgment. "Three of the humpers, painted head to toe in man-eating war paint. Spikes on their head, spikes on their elbows, spikes on their mother-humping asses. They've got their spears pointed right at me, yelling cannibal scat, about to cook me up. I say, 'Hey, you haven't really eaten until you've tasted the best man flesh there is.' The first cannibal says '*Uga buga*, what that?' I say 'other cannibal.' He looks all confused, but then shrugs and slices off his friend's ear, takes a bite, and smiles. 'He right! Taste great!' His friend, one ear all bloody and cut to pieces, takes his knife and slices off the third one's nose, and eats it. 'Yeah! Yum!' The third one, seeing how good cannibal seems to taste, takes his knife and slices off the first one's tool. He pops it in his mouth and grimaces. 'This taste like scat!' I look at the first one and say, 'That ear tasted great right? That's 'cause cannibals love to hear each other talk! Now go find some more cannibal ear to eat!' He nods, and walks away, looking for more ear. I look at the second one and say, 'And that nose, that tasted yummy, right? That's because you cannibals love the way each other smell! Now go find more cannibal nose to eat!" He smiles and runs off into the swamp to find him some more nose. The third one is looking real confused now. So I turn to him and say 'And his tool, it tasted like scat, right?' He nodded, 'Uh huh!' 'That's cause you dumb mothers like to hump each other up the ass. Now go find your two friends and get to it!'" Hakkida and Gensoarato laughed loudly. Fisherbird smiled uncomfortably and looked over at Tianati again. The giant did not laugh.

"I can never understand what makes you Littles laugh. That's the dumbest joke I ever heard."

Checko laughed more. "Let's hear what makes you big humpers laugh," he said.

"Doing your little women and hearing them moan for the first time from a big tool." This made the others laugh even more. "I've had it; I'll see you clowns in the morning," the giant said. He shuffled away from the fire.

Checko turned to Hakkida. "What are your people like? I don't think I've heard tell of your town."

Hakkida paused and looked at Fisherbird. Tianati thought it was a warning look. "We're a simple folk. We fish and hunt. There are four villages with one chief, Chief Fogg. Our women are stout and hard-working."

Tianati stayed silent, watching Fisherbird's face for clues. But Fisherbird looked down at a small piece of wood he was whittling methodically.

"Wide women are good women. My own wife is kinda skinny. I keep telling her to put some meat on her bones." Checko laughed, and then looked at Gensoarato. "What of this chief of yours? Will he give us any trouble?"

Gensoarato said nothing. "No," said Fisherbird, without looking up from his whittling. "Fogg just tries to grow his corn and service his wives."

Checko looked over at Fisherbird, then back to Gensoarato and Hakkida. "Is this boy a friend of yours? He seems a little . . . different from you two."

Gensoarato spoke quickly. "He joined us a few years back. His own village moved far inland. They had trouble growing corn. But Fisherbird wanted to stay near the ocean."

Tianati watched Fisherbird. His whittling paused for just a moment at Gensoarato's words, but then resumed. *I've got to find out his story,* Tianati thought. "I'm calling it a night," he said. He found a spot away from the fire where he could lie on his side, his back to a large tree trunk, and keep an eye on the others. He did not go to sleep.

☽ ● ☾

The morning was again hot and muggy. Even before the sun was up, they were on the path to the Manatattos village. Gensoarato led the way, followed by Fisherbird. Checko and the giant followed close behind. Tianati lagged further back, but Hakkida stayed in the rear. Tianati was increasingly worried about the Manatattos' intentions, but he was unsure how he would get Fisherbird to open up. Then a rustling noise a few hundred yards to the right of the path caught Tianati's attention. He saw a scrawny doe startle away. This was his chance. "I'm going to get her," he said to Hakkida, and bolted off the path after the deer.

Hakkida called out "don't!" but it was too late; Tianati was off.

Fisherbird ran after Tianati, calling back to the others, "I'll help him."

123

Tianati ran as fast as he could, but he had no intention of catching the doe. He just wanted to get as far from the path as he could. He turned to see that Fisherbird had followed him as he'd hoped. After a good five minutes of hard running he stopped, letting Fisherbird catch up. "You alone?"

"No one else followed. They had to stay with your big friend."

"Suppose you tell me what the hell is going on."

"If you want to live, you'll get as far away from the Manatattos as you can. Leave your giant and the clown and they won't chase you."

"I can't do that. Why do they want the giant?"

"These people are greedy woman-stealers. Chief Fogg takes all the girls from all the villages in the area as soon as they're of age. He's made lots of enemies, and needs more and tougher fighters. He'll make your giant a slave and use him to scare the countryside into submission. I'm a slave. My sister was taken and is one of Fogg's 'wives.' If I so much as step out of line, he'll kill her. Now I have to get back. If you're dumb enough to come back, I suggest you bring that deer meat to douse Hakkido's suspicions. He already thinks you're up to something." Fisherbird set off toward the path, calling over his left shoulder as he broke into a jog, "Oh, and the small one, Gensoarato, is a great shot with the atlatl. Get him first."

>●C

It took Tianati some time to track the deer, and even longer to find the path again. It was late afternoon before he caught up with the Manatattos. "Care to eat?" He tossed the deer down.

Hakkido snorted. "We've lost a lot of time. We'll have to camp again tonight before getting to the village."

"At least we'll eat well tonight. Giant, help me carve this beauty up," said Ti.

The giant came over and pulled his knife out. "I'll get the small parts," Tianati said, making eye contact with the giant as he began to clean the smaller innards. "I need you to take out the big part."

The giant nodded as he started removing the heart. "Did I hear you right? You want me to take this?" He held up the heart, his arm pointing towards Hakkido. Tianati did not answer with words. He simply launched his knife through the air right at Gensoarato, who did not see it coming. Gensoarato went down with a knife to his neck while the giant's long blade flew through the air at Hakkido, hitting him squarely in the belly. The giant left nothing to chance, leaping over to the dying Manatatto to finish him with a twist of his neck. Tianati went to the smaller one and pulled his knife from the young man's neck, torqueing it to make sure he was dead. Ti looked around. Fisherbird was nowhere to be seen.

"What the hell?" said Checko, who had barely moved during the brief melee.

"Fisherbird told me these guys were going to take the giant as a slave. They are woman-stealers. He's a slave himself. His sister is Chief Fogg's hostage, so he may be forced to tell the chief about us. We better get out of here. Checko, any idea which way to Zialand?"

Checko laughed. "Zialand? The best way is back to the sea. At least we know where to get a raft!"

The giant laughed too. "These punks would never have made me a slave. And if you think I'm getting back on the water, you're dumber than I thought."

"We don't have a choice," said Tianati. "Look!" He pointed to the Western horizon. Smoke signals rose and drums could be heard. To the south, answering smoke began to rise and more drums could be heard. "This whole countryside is about to come right at us. Time to see how fast Checko can run!"

He set off at a good pace back down the path. Checko took off right after him. As the drums grew louder, Tianati looked back to see the giant grudgingly following, a frown still stuck on his face.

$$\mathbb{)} \bullet \mathbb{(}$$

They were lucky to be running under a gibbous moon, and kept going straight through the night. Tianati was weary after two days of traveling without rest, but he knew their safety depended on speed, and pushed himself onward. The giant, with his long legs, easily matched Tianati's pace, and prodded Checko to move faster, threatening to leave him behind if he didn't. They made it to the raft on the beach before dawn, and without delay pushed off into the bay. Their good luck held, as a strong breeze blew off the land, pushing them out quickly past the mangrove barrier islands into the sea.

The wind held the whole next day, pushing their stolen raft far down the coast. But that night it died. They paddled until exhaustion took over, and slept as the dawn broke windless and muggy. In the weak morning light, Checko spotted two canoes, manned with five Manatatto warriors each, paddling hard toward them.

"Ten against three is no good," he said, "but if we could flip one of those canoes over we could make it a fair fight."

"That's your job, Checko," Tianati replied. "If you can get them in the water I've got plenty of darts. And giant, did I see you gathering rocks back at the beach?"

The giant pulled a large sack out from the back of the lean-to. "I can do some damage with these," he said, smiling.

"OK, just make sure you don't hit me," said Checko and reached into a bag of his own to pull out a strange-looking gourd tube, long and curved with holes on both ends. He then grabbed a heavy stone and tied it around his waist with a leather cord, crouched down behind the lean-to out of sight of the approaching Manatattos, and slipped into the ocean. Tianati and the giant watched in wonder as the tip of the gourd moved around the raft and stopped about twenty yards away, in the path of the oncoming canoes.

"I'll be damned," said the giant, "that clown is full of surprises."

"Let's give him some cover," said Tianati, and he started hooting and shouting insults at the Manatattos. The giant followed suit, and soon a few of the warriors stood up in the canoes and loaded their atlatls, preparing shots to test the range. Tianati tried very hard not to look down at the tip of Checko's gourd, but he could see out of the corner of his eye that the lead canoe was getting very close to Checko's underwater hiding spot. The giant threw his first rock, deliberately aiming beyond where Checko floated, and scored a hit on the second canoe. Atlatl darts started flying at the boat and Tianati returned fire, narrowly missing the warriors in the first canoe.

Then Checko did his part. The first canoe tipped over without warning, dumping the warriors into the sea. Tianati refrained from raining darts on them, worried he'd hit Checko by mistake. The giant was less reluctant, and cracked two Manatatto skulls with rocks. Checko, miraculously, was still undetected by the warriors, and managed to up-end the second canoe as well. His part done, he swam to the raft as fast as possible. As soon as Checko was safely away from the canoes Tianati and the giant rained darts and stones down on the heads of the confused and exposed warriors, killing them in only a few minutes.

"We better get some distance from the bodies," said Checko, "the sharks will be here in no time." The giant needed no further prodding, and began paddling furiously. Tianati could already see fins circling the upended canoes, and the water beginning to churn.

ELEVEN

HOME BREW

Sweat ran down Apeni's bare arms, making the handle of the long wooden spoon slick. She exhaled deeply and took a break from stirring to lift her head and wipe her brow. It was a cool autumn evening, but making groshi was hot work. She knew this would be her last chance to brew a good batch before her best friend Franchanga's wedding, and she wanted to make sure she had brewed it just right. She dipped her tasting spoon in, blew on the hot brew, and took a tiny taste. Almost there, she thought. Another night to let it sit and this batch would be good enough for a wedding. She covered the large clay pot and stepped outside to cool off. A group of teenaged boys played ball games in the square, while the local Astronomer chatted with her uncle Tanteno on the steps of the temple mound. The sky was bright blue and the air smelled of fallen leaves and cooking fires.

She walked over to the house where her cousin Hellerian lived, and knocked lightly on the door frame. "Hallo?" she called.

"Apeni! Come in cousin, come in!"

Apeni walked into the small wood-framed house, gave Hellerian a hug, and sat cross-legged on the floor. "I think I've got the groshi nearly done, finally."

"Good," said Hellerian. "The girls' dance is ready too. I just hope Ginni doesn't trip over her own feet!"

Apeni laughed. "Not nice, Heller." Her smile disappeared. "I wish Tianati could be here. He loves my groshi."

Hellerian looked at her with concern. "Have you heard any news?"

"No. But I don't expect to. He must be half way to Zialand by now."

Hellerian changed the subject. "I bet Garank shows up." She winked at Apeni. "He will invent some excuse," she deepened her voice in a clownish imitation of Garank, "'I've got to deliver an important message to the frontier, Mr. Astronomer,'" and laughed.

Apeni smiled despite herself, but she doubted Garank could make it. He'd been tapped to serve on the High Guard, the elite group of warriors who protected the People's Council. She knew from his last message to her that the People's Council did not give members of the High Guard leave absent exceptional circumstances. Besides, she was probably the furthest thing from his mind, surrounded by all those city girls with their fancy hair and flirty ways.

"Apeni! Apeni!" a young boy from the village named Kiltin called from outside. Apeni stood and poked her head out the door. The boy was running her way, tiring from what looked to have been a long run. "Apeni," he said breathlessly, through a big smile. "Someone is coming to see you!"

"Who?" She dared not hope it was Garank.

"A stranger. A girl. She's coming up the path now, look!"

Down the road Apeni saw a slim wisp of a girl, hair cut short, her youthful face weary but determined, walking briskly into the village. The boy waved his arms over his head to get her attention, calling out, "over here! She's over here!"

The girl walked up to Apeni, her round wide green-flecked hazel eyes boring into Apeni's own deep dark browns. A grin spread across her face. "You have his eyes!" She said.

"What?"

"I'm sorry, I am being rude. I am Naamani, from the lands of the great eastern ocean. I come with news of your brother, Tianati, and to give you this." She handed Apeni the old child's bead story she'd carried all the way from Mouth City.

Apeni cried and smiled, and reached out her arms to give Naamani a deep hug. "Oh thank you, thank you. Tell me, is he well? When will he return?" the words rushed out.

"When I left him he was alive and well, but that was months ago, and he still had far to go." Naamani didn't mince words. "He was still with . . ."

Apeni interrupted her, "now I am the rude one! Come with me, you must be tired and hungry. We'll sit, rest, eat, and then you can tell me your story!" She grabbed Naamani's slim hands and led her, half running, half skipping, across town back to her house.

☽ ● ☾

It took Naamani most of the day to tell Apeni all that had happened. When she told Apeni how Tianati had freed her at Mouth City, Apeni cried, saying, "he's a good man. But why did you come back here? Why not send a messenger like Tianati said?"

Apeni took a deep breath. "When the Allegh took me aside to say goodbye, he whispered something terrifying in my ear. He said 'do not return to the People's lands. Promise me you'll stay far away from the People's lands.' And I promised him. I lied."

Apeni stared at Naamani's firelit face. They'd been talking for hours, and though it was already past midnight, neither showed any sign of sleepiness. "What do you think will happen?" she asked again.

Naamani shrugged. "I wish I knew. That giant is hard to read. I do not think the Allegh trust your People at all. And I don't blame them." Apeni looked hurt. "Sorry Apeni. There are just so many of you, and not all of you are good."

"They mean to break the peace, start the war anew," she said. "That's why the Allegh told you not to return to our lands, isn't it?"

"I think so," Naamani said. "At least, I thought so enough to come tell you."

"Why did you lie to him? Why did you risk your life to come here?"

Naamani stared into the fire for several minutes before answering. "Your brother was kind. One of the good ones. He freed me. I felt I owed it to him, to you, to warn you. And I don't want the Allegh to . . ." she stopped.

"Don't want the Allegh to . . . what?"

Naamani had tears in her eyes. "I . . . love him," she whispered.

"Tianati?"

"No, Apeni. The giant. The Allegh. I love him." Her voice grew stronger. "And I will not have your blood on his hands."

TWELVE

PITZ

The weather cooperated as they sailed south. A steady north breeze pushed them over calm warm seas along a monotonous mangrove coast. After a few weeks they began to see other sailing rafts and canoes, most of which ignored them. Occasionally a trader would hail them with a greeting. Checko spoke the local trading tongue, and answered in kind. Tianati checked his map every day, and when the moon turned dark again, he asked Checko to start asking traders for the Owl River. His map instructed that the best way to the capital of Zialand was to head up the Owl River—known as Tukul River to the locals, after their word for owl—to a large trading city near its mouth. The city, at least at one time, had had a large contingent of the People living there in exile. If Tianati could find this city he could learn the current state of affairs in Zialand and begin the final leg of his mission.

Over the calm, slow days of sailing, Tianati asked Checko to teach him the basics of the local trading tongue. Tianati was good with languages, and soon had a working ability to understand Checko's conversations with the locals.

"Hallo, friend!" Checko hollered at a passing raft.

A tall man with an elaborate hat and jewelry answered back from the raft "Hallo traveler! What do you seek?"

"We're looking for the Tukul River. Can you help?"

"You're a good two or three days from its mouth. Look for the *tsaab tsan.*"

Tianati could not understand the last words. Checko also seemed to have difficulty with them. "What are *tsaab tsan?*" Checko asked.

The man laughed. He said the word *tsaab* slowly and loudly, holding up two fingers. Then he said *tsan,* and began moving his hand in the wavy motion universally understood to mean "snake," while hissing loudly.

"A snake. Look for the two snakes," Tianati said to Checko.

"Thanks, genius. I never would have figured that out," sneered Checko. The man on the raft was still laughing. Checko shouted a thank you and turned to Tianati. "Listen, I'm going to have to leave you after we find these two snakes. You think you and the giant can handle it from here?"

The giant had been watching all of this in amused silence. "Hey Checko, I never thought I'd say this, but I'm going to miss you, old clown."

Checko grinned. "You know where to stop for dinner on your way back."

"Have you heard whether the overland road is a safe way back? How far inland do you think those Manatattos control?" asked Tianati.

"There is a trade route that runs well west and north of any Manatatto towns, I'm sure. I know goods make their way on that road, but I have no idea how safe it is. Is any road truly safe?"

"No. Would you tell any children of the People you see on their Missions that we made it at least this far?"

"Of course. I hope you don't mind if I ask for some more of that great smokeweed in return."

☽ ● ☾

For the next two days the coastline was crowded with towns, and the sea was teeming with boats. Smoke from countless fires rose all along the coast. On the third day they came to the mouth of the Tukul River. A forty-foot-high stone and wood tower built to resemble two intertwining snakes stood at the point where the river met the sea. But they would not have missed the river even without the tower. Hundreds of small- and medium-sized craft clogged the opening in a chaotic but flowing dance. "I'm not going in there," said Checko, "they may tax me for my boat."

Tianati was surprised. "You have to pay for taking a boat up the river?"

"See those bright red flags flying on all the sailing vessels? And the green ones on the canoes? Those are issued by the city up the river—the place you're headed—and they cost money. If you don't have one, you can't go upriver." He pulled the raft up to a beach a few hundred feet from the snakes. A cluster of trading shacks sat under the palm trees. "As soon as I find a little chocolate for Sherriancha I'll say goodbye, my friends."

Checko grabbed a bag of spicy gator jerky to use in trade and headed off toward the traders. He soon returned with a bag of dark beans, and set about refilling his water from a nearby stream and preparing the boat for push-off.

Tianati pulled out a handful of his dream mix, handed it to Checko, and said goodbye. "Remember us when you smoke!"

The giant slapped Checko on the back a little too hard and laughed. "Watch out for cannibals!"

Checko wasted little time in turning the raft back north. Tacking against the wind, he slowly moved out of sight.

"Well giant, time to meet the locals."

"I hope Checko taught you the tongue right. Don't go calling some chief a chick by mistake."

$$\text{)} \bullet \text{(}$$

They followed the road that ran along the river until they found the city walls. Guards with armor and weapons that appeared more showy than effective stopped them at the gate.

"We are here to trade," said Tianati, as carefully and clearly as he could.

"Your names and nations."

"Tianati of the People who live on the Great Ohio River to the north."

"The Allegh who lives along the river of that name to the north," said the giant.

Tianati smiled. He knew a giant would never reveal his true name to anyone, much less a pompous city guard.

The guards looked straight ahead while stating in unison: "You are now subject to the law of the City of Toton. No fighting, no singing, no *pitz* without the written approval of the mayor, on penalty of death." They lifted their spears to let Tianati and the giant pass.

"I wonder what *pitz* is," whispered Tianati, when they were past the gate.

"No idea," muttered the giant, "but we better not do it! And no singing? What the hell?"

☽●☾

The city was unlike anything they had ever seen. Tens of thousands of people milled about, all seeming to have some urgent purpose. Sellers of wares yelled prices and insults from countless booths and tables. Huge, grotesque statutes peered down on them with threatening glares from towers and stepped mounds of stone. The ground was paved everywhere with even, flat rock. The air was filled with smells both foul and enticing. Meats Tianati had never seen turned on spits. Spices he had never dreamed of filled his nostrils. Smoke curled out of thousands of roofs.

And the women. Skin so creamy and brown Tianati could not help but stare. These women had breasts larger than he was used to up north, as well as long legs and exotic eyes. Tianati saw the giant staring as well. "Listen, we don't know their laws yet. We've got to stay away from the girls or our heads will end up on top of a spike. Come on, let's find some of my people."

They wandered down side streets for hours, until they found houses with the familiar decorations of the north. Tianati called a welcome at the nicest of the homes.

The door was opened by a boy of just over ten. "*Inic ou pico?*"

"Do you speak trader?" Tianati asked slowly, trying hard to speak the words correctly in the local traders' tongue.

The boy smiled. "It would probably be easier if we just spoke our own language!" he said in a thickly-accented People's tongue.

"Yes!" Tianati said, and smiled. "I've come from the north. I have stories to tell and smokeweed to share. Is your father home?"

"He's dead. My mother's at the market. You can come in, I guess, and wait for her."

Tianati looked at the giant and shrugged. "Do you mind if my friend comes in as well?"

The boy looked at the seven-foot-tall man dressed in strange northern furs, his skin burnt and tanned from weeks on the sea, his face bearing scars of years of war. "What's your name?" the boy asked.

"You can call me giant. What is your name?"

"Juntal. Are you really a giant?"

"What do you think?"

The boy grinned. "Wait 'til my mom sees you!"

Juntal's house was small but well-kept. There was only one room, and three beds took up much of the space along the walls. Tianati and the giant sat on the floor, eating some corn snacks the boy brought out. Juntal told them about his family and the city. "My mom Kaya and I moved here after dad was killed. We're close to the market where mom works."

"I am sorry to hear your father died," said Ti. "How long ago did it happen?"

"Three years ago. I was just eight. He died playing *pitz*."

Tianati looked at the giant. "What is *pitz*?"

The boy looked startled. "Are you joking? I've never met anyone who didn't know *pitz*." He paused as if to see if they were actually serious. "*Pitz* is only the most important thing in the world! It's the game of the gods, the sport of the kings, the ball game for all the people of the world!"

"It's a game?"

"A game! Yeah, a game. But not just a game. *The* game! Have you really never seen it? We have to go watch!"

"We're forbidden. We were told 'no *pitz*' or we would die!" Tianati did a pretty good imitation of the stiff guard at the gate.

Juntal laughed. "Everyone watches *pitz*. Everyone plays *pitz*. Everyone gambles on *pitz*. You won't get caught. Heck, this is Toton, not the City of the Gods. There's a court down the street. Come on, my mom won't be home for a couple of hours anyway."

The giant looked interested. Giants loved games, especially games on which they could wager. Tianati was not convinced. "I don't think it's a good idea. We're pretty conspicuous."

"Come on Tianati, we'll borrow one of Juntal's dad's old hats. I'll hunch over. We'll be fine. Juntal, would you be able to place a bet for me? But we'll need to trade some of our goods for money first. Where can we do that?"

Tianati had never seen the giant this animated. The Allegh's enthusiasm won him over. "OK, but at the first sign of trouble we leave, got it?"

"Yes, dad," said the giant.

Juntal laughed again. "Follow me. You have smokeweed, right? We can sell that at the market for cacao beans. You can bet with the beans and if you win more they can buy you anything you want."

The boy fetched a large, feathered headdress, which he perched on the giant's head. "There," he said, "now no one will notice you!" With that he ran out the door, leaving a bemused Tianati and a bedecked giant to follow.

☽ ● ☾

Tianati was able to get a hundred beans for a few pinches of his tobacco mix. The giant sold a copper toy boat Tianati had not even known he was carrying, and received an even larger handful of beans in return. Out of curiosity, Tianati asked a merchant how much a jaguar skin coat cost, asking Juntal to translate.

"That's a thousand beans, Tianati," said Juntal.

"I'll pass."

From the market they made their way to the *pitz* court. Tianati judged the court to be about sixty arms-lenths long and ten arms-lengths wide, running east-west. It was walled with four layers of large flagstone blocks, cut perfectly and with no blemish on them, save for at the corners and in the middle. There, elaborate carved blocks painted in colorful hues told the story of how the gods played *pitz*, as well as the terrible tale of how losers might forfeit their heads.

Stepped stone bleachers ran up from the walls on the north and south sides, and hundreds of spectators were already seated, waiting for that afternoon's match. Juntal led Tianati and the giant up a set of stairs behind the court to a stepped seating area on the south end. They sat toward the top, with no one behind them, to attract less attention.

"You should watch a game or two before making any bets, to get the idea of the game," Juntal said.

Tianati saw many spectators drinking a frothy brown drink that smelled of cacao and chilies. "How about something to drink?"

"I'll get a couple. You want *pulke* in yours?"

"*Pulke?*"

"Gets you drunk."

"Drunk?" said Tianati.

"Stupid."

"Who are you calling stupid?"

"No, it makes you stupid. People like it. Mom doesn't let me drink it yet. The guards would tell you it's not allowed, just like *pitz* is not allowed, except for the priests. But just like *pitz*, everybody does it."

"Maybe next time. Just make mine stupid-free." Tianati handed the boy a few beans. "This enough?"

"Perfect. Got it." Juntal scooted back down the stairs.

"You know, giant, this boy could be useful. He knows how things work around here, and we need a translator."

"We'll see if he brings me good luck. Then I can tell you how useful he could be."

Juntal came back holding three large mugs of the brown drink. "This is the best *yom cacao* in the city, I think."

Tianati took a sip. Some of the foam stuck to his lip. He wiped it off with the back of his hand. The drink tasted spicy and rich, and smelled of deep, brown, clean earth and gardens of magical spices. "Wow."

"Go slow," said Juntal, "if you've never had it before it might upset your stomach."

Tianati tried to sip slowly, but the drink was so good and so novel he had a hard time not gulping the whole mug down.

The giant had a different reaction. He took one sip, spit it to the ground, and said, "Thanks but no thanks, Juntal. When's this game of yours going to start anyway?"

"Now! Look!" Juntal pointed at the east end of the court.

Fires sprang up on either side of the court, and a man dressed as an eagle danced out. He played to the crowd in the north bleachers first, causing them to roar with approval, then danced over to the south bleachers, where the spectators around and below Tianati again roared in response. In his right hand, the eagle dancer held a clutch of spears. Drummers hidden somewhere nearby began a frantic drumbeat that picked up pace as the eagle dancer hurled his spears at the west end of the court.

In the north bleachers, a man stood. He was dressed simply, but looked important. He held a brightly-painted ball in his right hand and raised it above his head, to the cheers of all. The drumming suddenly stopped. A moment of eerie quiet passed before Tianati saw most of the spectators, including Juntal, pull small, pipe-shaped objects to their mouth. At once, sharp whistles at every pitch cut the air and the drumming resumed with a steady, slow beat.

A trio of men appeared at the western end of the court, walking slowly and deliberately. A moment later Tianati noticed that a similar group had entered the arena from the eastern end. At the west end the three players wore jaguar garb. They walked until they were even with Tianati's seat. The three players emerging from the east were dressed as some kind of lizard Tianati had never seen before. Tianati decided he wanted the jaguars to win, and it seemed that Juntal was also rooting for them.

The players met at the middle of the court and stared each other down as the drumming stopped. The man with the ball let out a loud, clear cry of *"Ti Pitziil!"* and threw the ball down into the court. Tianati was surprised to see it bounce like a frog when it hit the ground, but the players were clearly expecting this; the lead jaguar expertly moved to exactly where the bouncing ball was about to land and smacked it with a stone that was fitted over his hand like a glove. The ball bounced back towards the lizards, and the lead lizard deflected it with his hip.

The game unfolded strangely to Tianati's eyes, but after some time he perceived that the team that failed to stop the ball from hitting the wall behind it lost points, and a player who failed to return the ball before it bounced twice lost points as well. The more he watched, the more he realized that *pitz* was in many ways similar to a game he'd played as a child and watched hundreds of times in the ball courts of the People's City. The main difference was that here they played with a very bouncy ball using their hands and hips, instead of catching and hurling a hard ball with baskets on sticks, as the People did. But in both games the players battled to get the ball into the opponents' home.

Before too long, Tianati found himself cheering alongside Juntal as the jaguars began to show their superiority over the lizards. The giant didn't cheer, but he was watching with obvious interest. Soon the game was finished, but no one in the crowd moved to leave. In fact, an odd hush fell over the spectators. In the north bleachers, the man who had thrown the ball down to begin the match stood again and loudly proclaimed the jaguars the winners. He then commanded the losing captain to walk to the center of the north wall.

The ball thrower climbed down from the bleachers and stood beside the captain of the lizard team. Drawing a long, black knife from his belt, he pulled the losing captain's hair back and held the knife to the edge of the captain's throat. He paused and called out a question to the crowd. Tianati couldn't understand the words, but the import was clear. He was asking the crowd whether he should kill or spare the captain.

Beside Tianati, Juntal looked away from the field, staring silently at his own hands in his lap. Tianati remembered Juntal saying his father had died playing *pitz*, and wondered if it had been in a moment like this one, as the result of a loss. All around them people began to rise to their feet and call out a response to the ball thrower's question, while Tianati intently watched the loser, wondering what the spectators were demanding.

A moment later he had his answer. The ball thrower let go of the captain's hair and pushed him back toward the east end of the arena, where he danced out with arms raised up to the cheers of the crowd. Tianati breathed a sigh of relief and looked back at Juntal, who had his eyes on the field again.

"The next match will start in about five minutes," the boy said. "The jaguars will keep playing until dark, or until they lose, whichever comes first. They've only lost a few times this year, so most of the betting is on the score. A good bet would be to say the jaguars will win by more than five. My friend Bixta told me the next team they play has a captain with a badly bruised hip."

The giant had watched the first game in complete silence. "The jaguars won that last game by three, right?"

"Right," said Juntal, appreciation in his voice, "and the lizards are one of the teams who've beaten them this year."

"OK, can you bet ten of my beans on the jaguars to win by more than five?"

"Good bet, giant!" Juntal took the giant's beans and ran down behind the stands again. Just as the next game was about to start, he returned.

"Made your bet. You'll get twenty beans if you win."

"Let's go jaguars!" said the giant.

)●(

They spent the next few hours watching *pitz*, with the giant winning all but one of his bets, and Tianati losing both of the ones he finally made. Dusk fell as they made their way back to Juntal's house. Torches were blazing on every street corner, and large braziers carved with fanged spirit faces stood in the centers of the larger intersections, lighting the city's evening crowds with a flickering glow.

When they reached Juntal's house they found his mother on the front stoop, husking corn.

"Where have you been?" she said, looking at Tianati and the giant with a combination of caution and disapproval. Tianati felt guilty, though he could not exactly say why.

"Hallo, young mother of Juntal. We bring respect and greetings from the land of our People far in the north, and thanks for the help and assistance your fine son has given to two tired travelers."

"Hallo yourself. You should be careful in this town. The priests don't look kindly on strangers taking liberties."

"Mom, they're OK," Juntal said. "I just showed them the market and the ball court. They're on their way to the City of the Gods."

Juntal's mother looked at Tianati and the giant again.

"You can call me Kaya. I don't like strangers going about town with my son, breaking the priests' laws."

"But mom, everyone does it! I even saw Hakal's dad there."

"I don't care. The priests have been stricter this year. The corn festival is in two months and they want to make a good impression on the visiting priests."

Kaya looked up at the giant, her expression softening after she'd made her point. "You're a big one, aren't you?" She smiled and Tianati noticed that she was uncommonly attractive.

"My folk are all tall, but I am tall even for them." The giant's deep voice seemed almost gentle, husky. "I have noticed that your folk are all attractive. You are beautiful even for them."

Kaya blushed and turned away. "Juntal, go find us some good corn and *habi* peppers. We're going to have guests for dinner."

Tianati looked at the giant with a mix of admiration and jealousy. He had not yet seen him act so charming. "Let us use some of our beans for the food. Our big one here did quite well at the ball games today."

☾ ● ☽

Dinner was like nothing Tianati had ever seen, smelled or tasted. The colors and aromas and flavors of spicy peppers, rich chocolate, strange tropical herbs, fleshy cactus, and ingredients he had never heard of blended together to leave him stuffed and wanting more. Kaya was a fantastic cook. They learned a lot through the conversation, too. Kaya was of the same stock as Tianati, but from clans that had chosen not to migrate to the north centuries earlier. She spoke the same language as Tianati, but with a very different accent, and many of the words she used were new to Tianati. Luckily for Tianati, she was well-versed in the local lore, and had a good grasp on the current political situation. She did her best to brief Tianati on the history of the People in Zialand.

"When your stupid civil war with the giants started, we began to see the Exiles arrive. They came in small groups at first, then larger waves. Always some giants in the groups. Not many, but some. Many stayed here in Toton, but most went on to the City of the Gods, where there were fewer who knew how to practice their northern crafts and where they could get better money for their wares."

She had been looking mostly at Tianati as she told the tale, but now she turned to the giant with a sardonic smile and said, "You can't get a good pipe down here to save your life. Never mind trying to find a bead story." The giant had sat on her left, quite close, his leg touching hers, and he laughed in a most un-giant-like way at her comment.

He has no idea what a good pipe is, Tianati thought with a touch of bitterness. He was surprised he felt jealous of this giant flirting with some strange Zialander. But he did.

Kaya brewed some atsik. Tianati's bitterness began to fade at the thought of having his first good cup of atsik in months. From the smell of it, Kaya knew what she was doing. "Do you want some chocolate in your atsik?" she asked.

"I'll pass, if that's alright with you," Tianati said.

She handed Tianati a cup, offered a cup to the giant, who refused, and sipped it herself with a shrug as she resumed her tale of the refugees who had fled to Zialand.

"At first they did very well. Their crafts were popular, their music became a hit, and many even became priests. The giants too were accepted, at least at first. But the City of the Gods was entering a dark time. Crops had been declining for decades. The old ways were increasingly being ignored, and the influence of the People's astronomers and priests had waned. The People in many of Zialand's cities, including ours, consider the old ways a nuisance to be endured only in times of festival, or worse, a joke. Yet other, harsher, priests have grown in power. Servants of dark totems, their ruthless warriors hold sway over much of the land. The capital is still in the balance, but the scales are tipping to the evil ones."

Tianati thought a healthy disrespect of the priesthood could be a good thing; but he also understood that a weak priesthood might cause the People to lose the knowledge and wisdom that was, for Tianati, the priests' main reason for being, and that such weakness could open the door to the kind of ambitious men and women who would use the influence of religion to grab and hold political power. Among his branch of the People, the priesthood had long ago transformed into a somewhat more secular organization of Astronomers, which did a good job of preserving and enhancing knowledge but did not pretend to have a monopoly on understanding the gods. They kept the time, built and used the observatories, and recorded the history of the fires. To be sure, they still were pious, presided over ceremonies at the churches, and delivered the true names to each year's crop of nineteen-year-olds. But the notion that they were infallible and must be looked upon with unquestioning adoration had long since passed into the shell heap of history. From Tianati's standpoint, that was a good thing. Even the last remnants of the priesthood's authority over others chafed at him. But Tianati kept his thoughts to himself. Kaya was clearly conservative when it came to the priesthood, and Tianati wanted to be a good guest. And anyway, things were different in Zialand. A decline in the power of the priesthood could mean the end of the People as an influential force, if they were pressed in on all sides by ambitious competing priesthoods.

Kaya continued. "Things began to become uncomfortable for the giants first. Priest-warriors eager to divert attention from the food shortages and increase their influence began insinuating that the Gods were angry with the city because of the giants. They began pointing them out, first through derision and insult, and then by open accusation of evil. Soon the rabble of the City of the Gods, hungry and angry, began to drive the giants into the worst quarters of the town. Many of the People's exiles stuck with the giants, because the two peoples had already endured so much together. Many others abandoned them. Four years ago, a priest named Ghagalexta sought to distinguish himself from the other priests by calling for the sacrifice of all the giants. His thugs rounded up all the giants who didn't flee and rolled their heads down the steps of the Snake Bird's Temple. The giants' remaining allies among the exiles watched in horror, knowing they would be next if they stood in the way. Some fought, mind you, and they did damage to a good number of priests, but their numbers were far too small to stop the carnage." Kaya looked in the giant's eyes and put her hand on his knee. "I'm sorry."

"I've seen plenty of bloodshed from little people, believe me Kaya." He paused, becoming visibly angry. "Are there any of us left in that city?"

Kaya took a long time before answering. "Last year I would have told you that there would be little chance of finding giants in the City of the Gods. But Ghagalexta was too extreme for the other priests. They couldn't stop the slaughter, but when it was over they took care of Ghagalexta in their own way. They sent him on a mission to the South from which they thought he could not return. They sent emissaries to the exiles and the giants who had fled, promising safety and protection. Many of those who had left actually returned to the City. But they remain poor, oppressed, and afraid. And their numbers are small. I fear too that Ghagalexta's allies are increasing in power again. Some are whispering that Ghagalexta himself has snuck back into the City, and has assumed one of the priest's mantles. Another purge seems like a real possibility. It would be very dangerous for you to go there."

148

OOO

Kaya's story infuriated Berengial. He turned to Tianati. "If there are giants in that damned City we can lead them out. I'm not turning back now. I will not leave my kin to be slaughtered."

"Sounds like a bad idea to me," Tianati replied. He turned to Kaya. "I think the giant might be better off staying here a while."

Kaya nodded. "Going to the City of the Gods may kill you. Why not send Tianati on with your message? Or better yet, you both stay here and send a messenger. Toton has always been more tolerant than the City of the Gods. I know several fast young runners who could get there and back in half a month."

"We can't rely on a messanger," said Tianati. "But I could go alone." He turned to the giant. "If we go to the city together you might do more harm than good. If I go alone, I'll attract less attention, and do more to help both our people. I promise you, I'll do everything in my power to get your kin out of there."

Berengial sat silently, looking down, seething with anger, but also feeling deep guilt. *This Little is willing to deliver my message to save me, and I helped plot to destroy his people.* He knew it was too late to stop the plans the Allegh had hatched back in the lands of the Ohio. He remembered Naamani's tearful farewell in Mouth City. In hushed tones he'd warned her to stay with the Mandans and not return to the People's lands. He'd made her promise to stay far away from the People's lands. He still remembered her tearful whispered answer.

"Why would I ever go back to those slavers?" She'd asked.

"Just promise me," he'd whispered.

She'd looked at him curiously, seeing deeper into his soul than he'd wanted. "What's going on?"

"Promise me!" He had grabbed her harder than he intended. She flinched and started to pull away.

"When I am free, giant, I will go where I please." Naamani's expression had softened slightly. "But I've no love for Tianati's kin. They deserve whatever's coming their way. I'll stay away. For you." She'd hugged him deeply but quickly disengaged and turned away, denying him the chance to look in her eyes to judge the truth of her pledge.

Berengial's face dropped with an unfamiliar mix of sadness and guilt at the memory. *The Allegh warriors are probably even now slaughtering Tianati's kin, and he is offering to help save mine.* His guilt rankled him, and he found an irrational anger welling up within him. He looked down at Tianati. "You're not the only one with a duty," he snapped. "We're both bound to deliver the message. But even if I weren't, I wouldn't leave my people to the evil of those priests. I'm going to your City of the Gods." He could not help but notice that Kaya looked crestfallen, and realized he might be missing out on more than just safety by leaving Toton.

》●《

The next morning, Tianati awoke early to pack and begin the last leg of the trip. The giant was already up and ready to go. "Did you really think I would let you have all the fun?" the Allegh said. He smiled, but in a very giant-like way—with a glint of the battle ahead in his eyes.

Tianati looked over at Juntal sleeping in the corner. "I wish he could come with us. He knows more about these people than we do— he'd be a big help."

"It's too dangerous. Maybe we can stop in and say hello again on our way back, if we make it out alive without hordes of spear-slinging giant killers at our backs."

They left Kaya and Juntal without making another sound.

THIRTEEN

CITY OF THE GODS

The road out of town was excellent and well travelled. Tianati and the giant had no problem making good time, and the beans the giant had won bought them enough food to keep them well fed. Every few miles they would find a cluster of tents by the side of the road with vendors selling fresh fruit and roasted meats. No one threatened them, but when it came time to camp for the night they decided to be safe and camp on a sheltered hillside well off the road. Just as Tianati was starting to drift off to sleep, he heard steps approaching from down the hill, and saw a small torch bobbing towards them. Quickly and silently he loaded his atlatl and tweaked the weights. With his foot he prodded the giant into wakefulness. The giant turned to him without saying a word and grabbed his spear. Whoever was coming for them was about to learn what a giant's spear and a People's atlatl dart felt like passing through their body at the same time.

"Hallo Tianati! Hallo giant!" the voice of Juntal called up to them from the darkness. Tianati lowered his atlatl. The giant frowned.

"You shouldn't have come," said the giant. "Go back to your mother. She'll never forgive us if you come with us into danger."

"I'm eleven years old, giant, and will be a man soon. Mother never told me about the slaughter of the giants. Now that I have a giant as a friend, I can't let more be killed. What kind of a man would let that happen?"

"You're still a boy," said Tianati, "and you must listen to your mother. She knows what's best for you."

"I won't go back. I'll follow you all the way." The boy looked determined, his thin jaw set.

The giant glanced at Tianati. "If he were a giant boy, I'd smack him 'til he was unconscious and leave him in the dust. But I don't know the ways of the People when it comes to insolent children."

"He knows this road better than us. If he's determined to track us I doubt even your beatings could keep him off our trail for long." He worried for the boy's safety, but no place was truly safe, he supposed. "And we could use an interpreter and a guide." Tianati turned to the boy. "If we let you come with us, you must return to your home when we tell you. We may need you to be a messenger while we take care of business in the City of the Gods."

The boy burst into a big grin. "Yes sir!"

The giant frowned even more deeply. "Your mother won't be happy about this. You better not die, boy."

☽ ● ☾

Juntal soon proved invaluable. He could read the road signs and negotiate with the vendors. He made their travel easier and less conspicuous. After just seven days of fast westward marching, they began to approach the outskirts of the City of the Gods. The road, which had followed the contours and rhythms of the terrain for much of their journey, became spear straight, and pointed at what Tianati thought was a small mountain or large foothill, around which thousands upon thousands of smoky fires burned.

"The City is straight ahead," said Juntal.

"By that hill?" Tianati asked.

Juntal laughed. "That's not a hill. That's an observatory!"

Tianati squinted in the bright light. Sure enough, the sides of the hill were straight and perfect. They had to be a day's march away, but he could see the clear edges of an immense pyramidal structure. He had heard stories of the scale of construction in the City of the Gods, but even the old men's tales didn't do justice to the massive size of the observatory.

The giant seemed anxious. He turned to Juntal. "When was the last time you were in the city?"

"My mom and I go every year to buy spices for the Feast of the Bats. You can get chilesque in Toton, but mom says it doesn't make stew like the City-bought chilesque. I don't like the stew much myself, but . . ."

"Tell me more about the city priests and their warriors," interrupted the giant. "What weapons do they carry?"

"The city has regular guards who carry clubs and shields. They're everywhere—at the gates, most busy corners, the important temples, the market. There are hundreds of different sects, each with its own head priest. Each sect's priest has his own personal warriors. Some of the priests' warrior corps are small and carry only clubs. Some number in the thousands and carry bows, spears, atlatls, and long blades. The best of the warriors fight for the Snake Priest. There are only three hundred Snake Priest warriors, but they're the strongest men and the best fighters. They carry only one weapon, a *macana*—it's a strong stick as tall as a man, covered on all sides with sharp blades made of obsidian. They wear tough knitted armor and large helmets." Juntal had a gleam in his eyes.

153

Tianati smiled. When Juntal spoke of the warriors he sounded like an old teacher — the smallest technical detail at his command. He imagined that every boy within a thousand miles of the City dreamed of becoming a Snake Priest warrior.

"This *macana*, have you ever seen it used in battle?"

"No," said the boy, "but they say it can take a man's head clean off with one blow."

"So can this," said the giant grimly, holding his own club menacingly aloft.

Juntal looked scared.

"Let's try to keep all of our heads right on top of our necks, alright?" Tianati said, grabbing the boy around the neck and pushing him up the road. "And let's get into this city of yours before dark. I don't want to encounter these snake-hissing head-cutters out here on the road on a moonless night."

☽ ● ☾

They came before the city gates just as the afternoon faded into dusk. The city was already fully lit, with elaborately-carved stone braziers burning on nearly every corner. No guards barred the entrance to the city. Too many travelers came and went to check everyone, and the gates had the look of ornament, not barricade. The giant drew looks, but no guard or warrior challenged the three travelers as they moved into the City of the Gods.

Tianati tried very hard not to gape, but he was overcome with wonder. The City of the Gods made the People's City seem like a scruffy hill village. A hundred of Juntal's town of Toton could have been swallowed within the city's walls. The streets were laid out in precise and elaborate patterns. At first Tianati thought they might get lost among the endless warren of streets and canals, but he eventually realized that all of these byways led inexorably towards the city core. There they found a mile-long central plaza, lined on two sides with extravagant temples and massive pyramids, and capped on the northern end with a pyramidal observatory. In any other city that observatory would have dominated the scene. But here an even larger structure — the huge pyramid they had spotted from miles away — anchored the eastern side of the plaza.

The plaza itself was full of wonders on a more human scale. Everywhere Tianati looked he saw merchants in booths hawking wares of all varieties, each booth uniquely outfitted and adorned by its owner. One booth was draped in purple cloth and shaped like a hunting tent; a small man sat cross-legged in front with his eyes closed, a brazier on a tripod at his side exhaling sweet-smelling incense. A wooden post with carvings announced to the literate what was for sale within this establishment, but to Tianati the symbols were meaningless. Further on he saw a large open tent functioning as a cafeteria, with a long line out into the street and tables inside packed with happy patrons. The smell of cooking meats and chilies made Tianati's mouth water. Performers of all sorts sought to entertain with dances, songs, jokes, and bizarre feats.

At one particularly busy corner, a man stood atop a pillar of stone, holding forth with a sharp tongue and answering any questions flung from the crowd. Tianati, the giant and the boy stopped to listen to him talk of the weather; Juntal whispered a quick translation.

"Some will say the gods are angry at our excess, punishing us for our lack of piety with drought and lost crops. But I say if the gods punished indecency with famine, our fair city's whores would not be so fat!"

The crowd laughed, but one woman shouted at him angrily. "How do you explain the lack of rain then, wise man?"

The man looked seriously down at the woman. "Fine lady, I no more understand the way clouds make water come down than I understand how women make men go up–if I knew either answer I would be ruling the world, not shouting from a rock!"

The crowd roared again. Tianati smiled too, but motioned to the others to move along. "We need to find the People's quarter. Juntal, any idea how to get there?"

"I think so, but every time I've come I've just followed my mom. I think it's to the northeast, past the big observatory."

It took the better part of an hour for them to make their way through the crowded city and the narrow streets of its neighborhoods to the quarter where the People congregated. Tianati saw a clear distinction between the homes in the People's quarter and those of the adjacent neighborhoods. Each of the People's homes bore a unique copper plate over the door, identifying the family that lived within. None of the homes in the other neighborhoods they had passed through had been marked with copper, though every neighborhood had had its own unique style.

"Juntal, do you have any cousins we can impose on?"

"Well, most of our kin have left the city for the hills, according to mom. But we used to have family down this street here." He pointed down a leafy side street lined with rows of flowers and small braziers. They approached a small stone house at the end of the street, and Juntal studied the copper nameplate on its door.

"Some of our family still live here," he said, "the Teons." He called into the house, "Hallo, cousins!"

A trim older woman with steady brown eyes and black and white hair tucked into a bun emerged from somewhere in the rear of the home and greeted them at the door. She smiled when she saw Juntal, but her eyes quickly flickered over the giant and her smile fled. "Nephew, it is a joy to see you of course," she said, speaking in the same heavily-accented version of the People's language that Juntal spoke. "But why do you bring trouble to our home?" She pointed with a suddenly shaking hand at the giant.

"Aunt Deeka, these are my friends, Tianati of the People, from the lands far to the north, and a giant, also from the north. They have come a very long way to deliver a message."

"They have come for nothing. Folk here are not interested in news from afar. We're trying to hold our own lives together. And a giant here will bring ruin on our home."

"Aunt, please. We have nowhere else to go, and I can't abandon my friends. Can you let us stay here for just a few days? Please?"

Deeka looked up and down the street as if worried that people were watching. She pulled Juntal close. "Listen Juntal, get inside quickly. You will do what we say and leave when we say you must leave. Now all of you, get in here."

The house was larger inside than it appeared from the street. Juntal explained to Tianati that two dozen relatives lived there in a series of interconnected suites united around a common courtyard. A coffee tree grew in the middle of the courtyard, and on the north wall fresh water bubbled up from hidden pipes into a white stone basin. Several young children played a game on the ground with small rubber balls and knobby wooden game pieces. Tianati heard the sound of a flute-pipe playing a pleasant slow tune from one of the back rooms. Two young girls busied themselves preparing vegetables and herbs next to the cooking hearth on the side of the courtyard opposite the basin, chatting happily. Everyone looked at the newcomers as they walked in. The girls squealed and ran to hug Juntal. The children stared up at the giant.

"These are my friends, cousins. Tianati and the giant," Juntal said.

A tall, thin man emerged from the back room closest to the hearth, holding a curved wooden pipe. Tianati held up his hand in the traditional greeting. "Hallo native!"

"Hallo traveler." The man's voice was quiet and steady. "What tales of the road can you share?"

The greeting was forced and formal. Tianati decided to dispense with the civilities. "My name is Tianati. The giant and I have come thousands of miles through peril and toil to bring a message to the People and the giants who live in this city. I need an audience with the Chief Astronomer so I can announce the news."

"Tianati, I am Harasha, the eldest of this home. Please, before we talk of your business, make yourselves at home. You can put your kits in the second room over there, then come sit with me out back while Juntal catches up with his cousins."

Tianati and the giant stowed their gear and joined Harasha on a small patio at the rear of the home. Harasha offered them a smoke and then sighed heavily.

"Tianati, you'll have a hard time gathering the People remaining in this city together in one place. And there is no 'Chief Astronomer' here anymore. He died—was killed. We're hunkered down in our homes, laying low while the priest clans carry out their pogroms on giants and friends of giants." He lowered his voice. "Many of us also protect giants. We have a tunnel system under this part of the city. Almost all of the living giants are hiding underground, waiting for a chance to escape. If we make trouble or attract too much attention all will be lost. The priests will ferret out our hidden sanctuary and kill all the giants."

The giant could not restrain himself any longer. "Take me to them."

"In good time, my large friend. Right now, we have to deal with you. Your passage through the city will not have gone unnoticed. It won't take long until some priest's warriors learn that you've come here. You must leave tonight." He paused and thought. "Ceti!" he called into a back room. "Ceti, come here please!"

A dark young man emerged from a back room. "Yes, uncle?" His face bore a look as if Harasha's summons had interrupted a far more important task.

"I need you to take these folks to the house on the canal. Wait until everyone is asleep and make sure no one sees you. The safety of our family depends on you doing this right. Can you do it?"

Ceti glared at his uncle. "Yes, sir."

Harasha turned to Tianati. "The house is in a far corner of the city. You must not come out of the house until we're ready. I'll arrange a meeting of the elders to talk about your message. You must trust me. Do not try to leave. Your lives are in danger, and the lives of our family are in the balance." He looked into the giant's face. "We'll do everything we can for your people. Be patient so we can do it right."

The giant frowned. "Patience is not one of my strengths."

☽ ● ☾

They shared a hearty dinner of corn and beans, with turkey legs fried in corn oil and coated in a rich chocolate sauce. As the children were being put to sleep, Harasha pulled Tianati aside. "There are five families of the People in this city that wield influence. We, the Teons, are one, but not the most powerful. The others are the Kikisommas, the Cahoks, the Madaks, and the Cherriskas. We Teons and the Cahoks are the most dedicated to saving the giants. The Kiksommas are weak and will go with the prevailing winds. The Madaks are the strongest family, and their elder, Hiathor, favors accommodating the priest warriors. He was the one who caused the death of the Chief Astronomer, though he denies it. If he had his way, the giants would be served up to the priests on a platter. The Madaks have been slowly winning over members of all the other clans, including my own. I fear that had you not arrived, all the giants would be dead before the end of the year. But maybe, just maybe, you could be the wild card. We must play you well, and carefully."

"Don't worry about the giant. He won't do anything stupid that would endanger his people."

"Perhaps. But if he thinks we've lost control of the council of elders, I suspect he may take matters into his own hands. And that would be disastrous."

"You worry about Hiathor. I'll take care of the giant."

$$\newcommand{\moon}{} \text{☽ ● ☾}$$

Tianati and the giant left the Teons' house well after midnight, accompanied by Juntal and Ceti. The moon was new and dark, and the city streets were nearly lightless. Only the dull glow of dying embers in the street-corner braziers gave any guidance.

Ceti was quiet and grumpy. He spoke only to give curt instructions and to urge the rest of the group to stay silent and close. He led them through a maze of back streets and alleyways, stopping at most intersections to listen for roaming guards. They saw no one for almost an hour, and Juntal relaxed enough to whisper to Tianati, "I think he's taking us the long way!"

"Shhh!" said Ceti angrily. "If I have to kill you to silence you I will, boy."

"Easy, young man," said Tianati to Ceti. "Let's just get where we're going."

Ceti glared at Tianati but said nothing. The giant smiled, but then his expression changed. "Someone's coming," he said in a deep whisper.

Ceti motioned Tianati and the others into a small side alley and mouthed *don't move.*

They did not need any prompting from their young guide. As they watched, a large contingent of Snake Priest warriors carrying *macanas* marched down the street, looking in all directions. Tianati tried not to breath. Without moving his head, he rolled his eyes to look at the

Allegh, who was barely out of the street. He wished the giant would try harder to hide. It almost seemed he was standing tall to attract the warriors' attention. They passed by without seeing him nonetheless. Ceti waited a few more minutes before whispering harshly, "Follow me, quickly."

The rest of the trip was tiring but uneventful. Less than an hour after seeing the Snake Priest warriors they arrived at the house on the canal. The outside was nondescript, a two-story stone structure that looked almost exactly the same as the ten other houses on the street. There was no copper plate over the door, no carvings on the wall, nothing to give the house a unique character. The neighborhood itself felt shabby, old, and a little unsafe. They went inside quickly. Tianati immediately noticed that, despite the house's rundown façade, the interior was well-appointed and spacious. There were actually four floors, not two, as it had appeared from the street. The entrance was on the second level, with a full floor below ground level and two floors above. In the back, the ceiling between the first and second floors had been removed, leaving a large two-story space with a cooking hearth, a round stone table big enough for fifteen to eat at comfortably, and windows looking out over a wide canal.

"I'm leaving," Ceti said abruptly. "Harasha will send a girl with food in the morning. She'll stay and help make the house comfortable. Don't leave and don't cause problems." He turned away and quickly walked out the door.

"Goodbye, Ceti!" the giant called out louder than he should have. Juntal and Tianati laughed despite themselves.

☽●☾

That night Tianati dreamed of falling, plunging past gnarled tree limbs, through thorny brambles, and onto a field of upright *macanas*.

He awoke in a sweat, got out of bed noiselessly, and walked to the large back room. Peering through the windows he could see dark houses on the opposite bank and the black, still water of the canal, almost invisible on this moonless night. Then he saw a movement in the water. A hand, and then a long, thin arm, slowly rose from the canal water; the bony index finger curled to point right at Tianati and a voice spoke to him below the level of hearing: *wicked, dirty birds must be thrown to the raccoons!* The arm descended back into the water but a head began to emerge, a decayed head with eye sockets visible and worms crawling though the remains of the nose. Tianati looked closer. It was his own face.

He screamed and awoke, panting and sweating. *Just a nightmare,* he thought. *Scat, I gotta get home.*

FOURTEEN

THE BURNING

Apeni woke up groggy. She was surprised to feel a heavy arm draped across her shoulders. A single blanket covered her and the body attached to the arm. *Garank,* she sighed. She noticed her breath smelled of groshi and her mouth was dry as dust. She lifted Garank's arm up slowly, trying not to wake him, and slipped out of bed. She tiptoed naked out of the tent and to the relieving place. She would be undisturbed. It was still early and none of the other celebrants were awake. Relieved, she washed up and drank deep from a bowl of spiced water, thinking about last night's wedding party. The ceremony had been nice, but the party had gotten crazy. Apeni thought that perhaps her groshi may have been brewed just a bit too potent. Her memory of the evening was blurry. She remembered singing and dancing and a great roaring fire. Franchanga had fallen into the river at one point. And somehow she'd ended up next to Garank in bed. As to that part of the night, she had no memory whatsoever. *Too bad,* she thought, *that's what I'd been dreaming of doing for years.* She quietly went back into the tent, put on a comfortable leather skirt, grabbed some dried berries and nuts, and looked down at Garank as he snored softly. She decided to take a walk and look for some herbs for breakfast.

Naamani was already awake and waiting for her outside. She looked anxious. "Apeni, now that you've had your little party for your friend, will you please listen to me and get out of this land?"

"Naamani," she sighed, "can you let me at least have breakfast before pushing for me to leave my entire world behind?"

"I fear it may already be too late. I am leaving tomorrow, with or without you."

Apeni sighed again. "Garank said the peace deal has been honored, and the Allegh are satisfied. They won't attack."

"You do not know how much they hate you. I hope you survive, I really do. I'm going to pack." She stalked back to her small makeshift tent on the edge of the wedding party camground.

The wedding had been held beside Point Town in the hilltop ceremonial complex that commanded a view of the confluence of the Allegh's river and the Crumblebank river. The wedding party had all camped nearby, forming a small makeshift village on the hillside. Most the residents of Point Town and many folks living in the villages of the northeast frontier had attended the wedding and the party, and the site bore the scars of the intense festivities. Three still smoldering bonfires were ringed with debris and the turf was beaten flat by hundreds of dancing feet. Apeni walked down the hill towards the banks of the Allegh's river, keeping the houses of Point Town to her left. On a small bluff over the river's edge she stopped and smelled the air. Autumn was in full swing, and the crisp air brought the smell of decaying leaves, along with a peculiarly acrid burning smell, unusual for this time of year. She looked upriver towards her hometown, then downriver, where Tianati had gone eight moons ago and low dark clouds crowded the horizon. During the war, she would often walk to the river and stare downriver, hoping to see her brother return but fearing him dead. But now she smiled, believing him safe. She fingered the small bead story in her pocket and thought back to the strange happy day last month when Naamani had brought her the good news that Tianati still lived and the ominous warning about the giants.

For weeks, Apeni had puzzled over Naamani's story. She thought at first the girl must be mistaken. But as her trust in Naamani's intellect grew she came to accept that the danger might very well be real. Shortly before Franchaga's wedding, Garank surprised her by returning from the People's City, saying the High Guard had released him for a month. Apeni told him Naamani's dire warning. He had laughed, and told her the Allegh were as determined to avoid more war as were the People. With an insider's assured confidence, he convinced her Naamani was just a naive former slave with little understanding of politics or war.

But now Naamani's insistence had her worried again. She stared far downriver and saw one, now two, now a dozen canoes. She briefly fantasized that Tianati was on one, but just as quickly knew he couldn't be. The canoes, of which she now counted more than thirty, were full of scores upon scores of giants, fully garbed for battle. Naamani was right! She turned and ran back to camp, calling Garank's name with alarm. The peculiar burning smell seemed stronger, and as she ran, trying to piece together what was happening, a grim thought popped into her panicked mind. *That smell is the smell of death.* "Naamani! Garank! Everybody wake up! Giants are attacking!"

Garank ran out from their tent, already holding his bow and arrows and strapping on his war belt. He shouted out hurried instructions to the other men, sending several to scout numbers and positions, and others to spread warnings throughout the northeast frontier towns. "Gather here in five minutes with everyone who can't fight, and make sure everyone's ready to run. Five minutes."

Naamani emerged from her tent, already packed and ready to run herself. She did not bother to gloat. "I'll get the bride and groom," she offered. Apeni nodded. Franchanga would have been in the deep woods with her new husband, as was the People's custom. With Naamani fetching Franchanga, Apeni was free to rouse and gather the guests and townspeople. After just a few minutes everyone in the town and wedding party was up and streaming to the hilltop. Apeni looked down to the confluence and saw that the Allegh war canoes were almost to the point. Naamani emerged from the woods with a very confused bride and groom in tow. "Hurry!" Apeni yelled.

Garank and several dozen strong young men were taking defensive positions behind hills and berms to hold the rear. "Apeni, run with all the speed you can for as long as you can to the crystal caverns near Red Fort. Wait there for us one night only. If we do not join you before sunrise flee south to the Smokey Mountains. The wild Chee Kees of the mountains are distant kin. They may shelter you awhile. Now run! Run!"

Apeni paused only long enough to kiss Garank quickly on his cheek, then led the gathered throngs in a quick jog up and over the steep hills and down into exodus while flames closed in on Point Town.

$$\text{☽ ⬤ ☾}$$

That night, the tired and shocked refugees huddled in the cold darkness of their cavern sanctuary whispering in hushed tones swearing vengeance on the hated giants. Apeni did not join in the quiet oaths. She was too worried about Garank to speak or sleep.

When the pale light of morning glimmered weakly through the cracks in the cave wall, she looked at the sleeping bodies of her people. As the light grew, she stood and looked for Naamani, but the slight girl was nowhere in the cave. As the people began to stir awake, she called Naamani's name, quietly at first, then louder. Finally a small voice answered, "Apeni! Over here."

But it was not Naamani. It was the boy Kiltin. "Kiltin, what is it? Have you seen Naamani?"

"Yes Apeni, I am sorry, but she made me promise!"

"Promise what? Where is she, Kiltin?"

"She left. I couldn't sleep so she and I played dice. Then she made me swear not to say anything until morning. She's left, Apeni. She's gone. She said don't follow her, you will not know where she's going, but she said she will make it better all alone. She said that you should go far south, and one day maybe she would find you again."

Apeni's face fell in sadness. She'll never make it past the giants, she thought, with tears in her eyes.

"She said one more thing," Kiltin said. "She said she knew Garank would return safe. And she said to make sure I told you not to cry."

Apeni smiled despite herself. She heard a sudden bustle at the cave entrance and turned with a start. "Garank!" she stood and rushed into his arms. He grimaced as she hugged him. "You're hurt!"

Garank smiled. "I'll live. Just got a club in the ribs." He lifted his vest to show Apeni a green and purple bruise the size of a fist. "See? It's nothing. But we've got to get moving. We think we lost them, but giants are great trackers. We've got to run harder and farther today than yesterday. If we can cross the mountain ridge and start heading down the other side we've got a shot." He raised his voice, "Let's go everybody, we need to start jogging NOW!" He looked back at Apeni again and smiled. "Hey, at least we're alive. I've got to apologize to Naamani. Where is she?"

Apeni frowned. "She left. Said not to follow her. I don't think she can survive out there alone."

Garank frowned too. "I don't know. There's a toughness in her I can't describe. If anyone can sneak past an army of giants, it's her. I bet she'll make it."

"Funny, that's what she said about you, Garank." She managed a small smile, grabbed her pack and headed out of the cave, already moving at a quick jog.

FIFTEEN

TIANATI'S WORD

The sun was bright by the time Tianati finally woke up. He heard voices downstairs and could smell fish frying for breakfast. To his delight, he also smelled good atsik brewing. He climbed down the ladder from his sleeping loft and saw Juntal already eating. A girl wearing a white sarong was cooking more fish at the hearth. She turned around when Tianati came down and smiled. Tianati felt something drop inside his chest when he looked into her pale grey eyes. Her whole face smiled but her eyes were sad.

"You must be Tianati," she said. "Hallo! I am Huaranshee. Uncle Harasha asked me to make sure you guys stay well fed and out of trouble."

"Hallo Huaranshee. Can it be that I smell atsik?"

She laughed. "Uncle told me you'd been traveling for some time. How long has it been since you had a good cup? Here you go." She poured him a large mug of steaming black atsik.

"Thank you; it's been too long." He sat beside Juntal and took a deep whiff of the atsik, watching Huaranshee over the edge of the mug. Her sarong swelled high and full over her large young breasts, the fabric thin enough that Tianati could see the outline of her nipples pointing up, seeming to smile at him.

She caught him looking her over and did a playful spin. "Like what you see, traveler?"

Tianati blushed despite himself, not knowing why she made him self-conscious. "Where'd you learn to make atsik like this?"

"My grandmother taught me when I was five. We still lived up north then. I remember the snow on the ground, the smell of burning oak and ash, and the smile on my grandfather's face when he tasted my first brew. It was terrible but my grandmother taught me throughout the winter how to balance the beans, nuts, and spices in just the right way." She turned back around to tend to the fish. "It's hard to find the right ingredients for good atsik down here, you know. It would be better if I made it up north."

"It tastes great to me."

She transferred a pile of crispy fish onto his plate. "Why are you here?"

Tianati hesitated. He wanted to tell her about the message, but his orders were to read the full text at once to the People in the city, and he did not want to do anything that might undermine the delicate political situation Harasha had described. If word of his presence leaked out and rumors started before Harasha had laid the groundwork with the right power brokers within the friendly families, it might be impossible to leave with a good number of the People, or with any living giants.

Juntal stood up from the table, interrupting Tianati's thoughts. "I'm going to fish off the dock," he called as he made his way out the back door.

Tianati looked at Huaranshee and decided, without much warrant, that he could trust her. "The war in the north is over. The Council wants the Exiles to return north."

Huaranshee turned back to him from the pan she'd been cleaning. "What made your Council think we'd want to go back to their snow-covered hills where boys play stupid war games? Anyway, there are so few of us left who have the will or the way to do anything grand."

Tianati sighed. "Looks like my job will not be easy. I'm supposed to persuade as many of the People as possible to return home, and bring the giants with them."

"Giants? There are barely any remaining alive in the city. As for the 'People' who live here, most are so aligned with the warrior priests now that they are hardly identifiable as the People at all. Hiathor and his Madak thugs barely pretend anymore; they are tools of the warrior priests, and the weaker families are starting to break. Those of us who have retained the old ways and tried to protect the giants have lost our homes, had our food stolen, and even been beaten. There are only about a hundred of us true People left. Will your Council be pleased if you drag a hundred refugees and a couple of giants into the Ohio valley? Is that what they had in mind?"

Tianati ate his fish without responding. Huaranshee went back to cleaning the pan. When she finished, she came back and sat down next to Tianati, close enough that her scent filled his nostrils. He felt himself becoming aroused. "Will your family, at least, come north with me?" he asked.

She put her hand on Tianati's leg and looked at him closely. "I don't know, traveler. But I have a feeling you and I are going to get to know each other well before that day comes." She stood and took his empty dish to clean it. Without turning around, she said in a low voice. "Come see me tonight, Tianati, once the house is asleep. I stay in the loft at the top of the house. We can talk together in low voices and figure out how you will succeed in your mission."

Tianati stared at the lithe, flowing curves of her back, her straight brown hair spreading down nearly to her waist, her thin but strong legs tapering up from delicate bare feet, and realized she was not a girl at all, but a confident young woman in full, grown and ripe and beautiful.

"Of course," he said.

>●(

Tianati spent the day constructing new darts for his atlatl, cleaning and polishing his tools and pipes, and restocking his kit. He appreciated the store of good straight wood, shavers and other wood-working tools, and quality point-stones in the house's dug-out basement. Harasha and his network of People opposed to the warrior priests must have planned for this house to serve as a base of operations for a possible rebellion, or perhaps a desperate last stand. He wondered if the same sort of narrow-minded fear and hatred that was fueling the slaughter of giants here in the City of the Gods was what had motivated his own nation's callous treatment of giants, leading to the decade-long war that had defined much his adult life. For the first time, he knew the People's Council had been right to send him on this mission. If the People were to survive, he had to succeed and bring the refugees and the giants home. The seeds of the People's demise were already germinated, and the peace would not last without a fresh influx of clear-eyed tolerance and open-heartedness from those who had seen the final fruits of hatred and division.

His thoughts drifted to Huaranshee. She had gone to the market to gather food for the coming days. He thought she could help him understand the dynamics of local politics in a way Harasha might miss. She had an empathy that saw beyond cold facts and postures. He would get as close to her thoughts and heart as he could—a part of his mission that he would enjoy very much.

When Tianati felt he'd created enough of an arsenal to last for the next month, he lay back on the soft, carpeted floor with his arms behind his head, and closed his eyes. He thought of Huaranshee spinning around again and again in her enticing white dress, and drifted into a pleasant afternoon nap.

》●《

When the afternoon sun suffused the canal house, Tianati found himself waking on the blanketed floor. Huaranshee was calling his name tunefully from the back patio. "Tianati! I could use a hand with the grill."

Tianati roused himself and shuffled out back. Huaranshee had been struggling to put a heavy stone grill atop the cooking pit, but had succeeded only in getting it propped against the side. Tianati yawned, scratched his belly, looked at the grill, and lifted it up in one smooth motion, trying to make the job look effortless. But the grill was much heavier than he'd guessed, and Huaranshee laughed as Tianati grimaced despite himself.

》●《

That night, after the remains of the dinner had been cleared and the rest of the household had fallen asleep, Tianati climbed quietly up to Huaranshee's loft at the top of the house. She murmured softly and opened her blanket for him. He saw that the white sarong that had so entranced him was gone, so he removed his own clothes as well and rolled under the blanket. She whispered in his ear, "You smell like the north," and nibbled on his earlobe.

"And you taste like the sun," he said, kissing her deeply.

She rolled onto her back and pulled him atop her without breaking the kiss, reached between his legs to guide him into her, and broke the kiss to gasp. She said his name quietly at first and then louder as he rocked in and out of her soft hot moistness. He moved his hands down to grab her firmly from behind while thrusting deeper into her and kissing her neck, lightly at first and then harder. Her words turned to moans as the tide rose in both of them for what seemed like an impossibly long time and then broke all at once in great rushing waves of pleasure. When they stopped moving she laughed the way only a newly satisfied woman can laugh, and said, "Just stay right where you are, I am not through with you yet." Tianati felt himself hardening again inside her.

Berengial spent the first two days in the house sleeping. All of his people loved to sleep for long stretches when possible, and he took full advantage of the opportunity presented by their confinement in the canal house. He missed breakfast on the first day, though the smell of frying fish briefly tempted him to stir. He slept through lunch and dinner and through the next night, missing breakfast and lunch again on the second day. He only awoke when he smelled roasting corn and grilling turkey. When he emerged from his cubby, he was surprised to see Harasha, Juntal, and an Allegh he had never met in the entrance to the house. Harasha looked older, somehow, and burdened. Tianati and Huaranshee came in through the back door from the grill to greet them.

Without waiting for formalities, Harasha spoke. "I'm afraid I bring grim news. Things have changed. Hiathor learned of your arrival, Tianati, and he thinks you're here to spark a revolt. To prevent you from succeeding he has taken the giants as his prisoners and moved them to a hidden prison under the Madak's control. He and his Madak goons plan to turn them over to the Snake Priest to gain his favor. They'll claim they have uncovered a traitorous plot, and I fear this will be the excuse the dark priests need to take control and purge the city of both giants and the remaining dissident People. Then it's only a matter of time before they round all of us up." He saw Berengial eyeing the strange Allegh curiously. Harasha turned to Berengial. "Ah, my Allegh friend, I have been rude. Do you know my other good Allegh friend?"

"I've not yet had the pleasure, Harasha. Will you excuse my use of our native tongue?"

"Of course."

Berengial shifted to the high Allegh language reserved for ceremonies to make sure only the Allegh could understand. "My name is Berengial, son of Berential and Fredenia, birthed in the valley of the beavers, tamer of six pumas."

The other Allegh answered in kind. "I am Khandrial, son of Khandriage and Larana, birthed in the hills of the Miski, tamer of one puma and three jaguars, and exile from the war against the People. I will get right to the point. Will you fight with us against the warrior priests of this godforsaken town to free our folk?"

Berengial smiled. "Nothing would make me happier than to crack open the skulls of these preening Littles." He clenched his fist over his heart in the Allegh sign of oath.

Khandrial did the same and smiled grimly. He shifted back to the People's tongue. "Harasha, we can trust these guys. Now where are our kin being held?"

"We don't know exactly where, at least not yet, but we will find out." He turned to Berengial and Tianati. "I'm sorry, but you'll have to wait here a while longer until we can find them."

Berengial growled and started to protest, but Huaranshee broke in. "Can't you eat while you plot?" She brought a platter of grilled turkey legs and set it on a three-legged stool in the center of the room. "Hallo, giant, nice to meet you," she said to Berengial, and executed a charming spin by way of greeting, her sarong floating out in a bewitchingly high circle.

Berengial was starving, and helped himself to a couple of turkey legs, but he didn't miss Tianati's reaction to the young woman's entrance. *He's hooked*, he thought to himself. "Hello Huaranshee. Have you already met my little friend Ti?"

Berengial smiled as Tianati glared at him, but Huaranshee laughed. She looked right at Berengial with a challenge in her flashing grey eyes. "He's not little to a tiny little thing like me, big man!"

Tianati quickly changed the subject. "Harasha, only a few people know of our mission, and other than us, they're all members of your household." Tianati let the implication hang in the air.

Harasha looked pained. "I fear that your suspicians may be well-founded." He paused, then said heavily, "I have not seen Ceti since he led you here."

Berengial grunted. "No surprise. He can lead our enemies to this house; we shouldn't stay here long."

"No," said Harasha, "Ceti may sympathize with the Madak's politics, and might give word of your arrival, but I can't imagine he would ever betray the safety of this house or his family."

"All the same," said Berengial, glaring at Harasha, "you need to find our people, and find them fast."

OOO

By the end of the third week in the house, the giant looked ready to tear the walls down. Tianati, on the other hand, found the time passed quickly, spending his days and nights with Huaranshee. Juntal and the giant resorted to spending most of their time on the back dock, fishing and talking. They were on the dock when Harasha finally returned, bursting through the door with a shout. "Tianati! Giant! Huaranshee! Juntal!" Juntal and the giant emerged through the back door and Tianati and Huaranshee rushed down from the loft, getting dressed. "We found them! Hiathor already turned them over to the Snake Priest, and they are in the prison under the Snake Priest's temple. I think I remember a back way in from my childhood, but we must go quickly if we're to have any chance of success. The streets are too dangerous for us. We must go by a dark and secret way. Gather your things quickly. We will leave by canal boat." He turned to Huaranshee and Juntal, "we all must go. The giant was right, it is no longer safe for us here." His face was pained. "Ceti has betrayed us."

Tianati repacked his kit and Berengial strapped on his weapons. Juntal handed everyone corn biscuits he'd bought at the market and saved for this occassion. They all went out the back door and boarded two long, thin canal boats docked behind the house. Harasha and Berengial were in the lead boat. Khandrial, Tianati, Huaranshee, and Juntal followed in the second boat.

Harasha led them down several back waterways to a narrow channel lined with high limestone walls that ran just behind the temples in the center of town. Berengial could run his fingers along the rock walls on both sides of the canal at the same time. The closeness was oppressive, and the windless heat was suffocating.

Berengial munched on one of Juntal's corn biscuits and tried to paddle without hitting the walls. "I hope you know where you're going," he said to Harasha.

"I haven't been here since I was a boy, but I'll never forget the way," Harasha replied. He pointed up the canal to where a gnarled old tree stump grew out of the wall, nearly blocking the canal. "Just past that tree there should be a cave opening on the left. That's where we're going."

They had some difficulty getting under the tree limbs. Berengial and Khandrial had to clamber out into the water and duck behind the boats to get past the twisted lower limbs. They found that the canal was so shallow they could walk with ease, and an opening appeared shortly past the tree, just as Harasha had remembered, so they did not bother to climb back in the boats. Harasha, at the front of the lead boat, reached the opening first. "Scat," he said. "This wasn't here when I was a boy. We'll have to get there a different way."

Berengial walked through the water to the opening and saw that it was gated with thick lacquered wood poles anchored in deep holes in the limestone walls. "Khandrial, come over here. Harasha, let us handle this." Berengial grabbed the end of one of the horizontal bars and Khandrial braced another end. With barely a grunt, they broke the gate open. Berengial smiled. "Never let a Little do an Allegh's job," he said.

$$\text{)} \bullet \text{(}$$

Harasha went in first, and sparked a flint to light a compact torch. Tianati climbed in after him. The cave floor was above the water line, but still damp. He didn't know how the giant would fit in the cave. But somehow both of the giants squeezed their frames into the narrow opening. The cavity opened up slightly just past the entrance, but it was still an uncomfortably tight fit inside. Harasha stopped at every fork in the cavern, trying to remember the route he had taken in his childhood. He finally gave up after about twenty minutes, as he faced two open passageways. "I don't remember this at all."

"Did you come this far when you were a kid?" Tianati asked.

"No. Some of these caves lead to the sacred mines below the big temple. Some lead to the priests' quarter, where the leaders of all the sects live. A few are special passages to individual temples. And there's a path to the prison, which I've heard of but never travelled to. I have no idea where either of these passages leads."

"When in doubt, go down," said Tianati. He started down the left-hand passage. Harasha and the others followed, the giants reluctantly. Ten minutes later, Tianati came to another set of embedded lacquered bars, and whispered back to the giant, "Hey, can you and your new friend pull these damn things off?"

The giants shuffled past Tianati in the cramped cave, positioned themselves on either side of the gated passage, grabbed the bars, and pulled the gate down. The corridor opened wider past the gate, so wide the giants could almost walk upright, and the whole troupe started jogging down the tunnel.

The giants saw the cells first and called out to the others. A long, low side cavern off of the main passageway was blocked off by a line of thick wooden bars reinforced with metal. Scores of miserable giants huddled behind the bars. Many stood when they saw their would-be rescuers.

"How are we going to break them out of here?" asked Tianati. No one had time to answer. Farther up the passageway, just past the bars, a group of men carrying obsidian-toothed *macanas* rushed towards them. "Snake Priest warriors!" Tianati warned, just in time, as the giant turned and ducked to avoid a swinging *macana*.

The giant had brought a large spear with him down the narrow passageways, and now he hurled it into the chest of the lead Snake Priest warrior, knocking him back along with four of his comrades, who fell against each other in the tight space. Tianati hurled three atlatl darts into the warriors before they knew what hit them. He saw a small stone fly past his right ear and strike a warrior in the forehead. *Juntal*, he thought with a smile, and reloaded his atlatl with another dart.

The Snake Priest warriors had had enough. They fled back up the passageway. Tianati and his party gathered before the cells.

"How are we going to open these cells?" Tianati said. The bars looked too stout for even giants to break.

"The doors are barred with long poles held in place at either end with knotted stays," said a giant from inside the nearest cell. We can't reach the knots from in here, but if any of you are good with rope, you should be able to untie them pretty quickly."

Tianati looked at the heavy wooden poles blocking the doors to the cells and saw the knots of thick rope holding them in place at each end. "Juntal, Harasha, you start working this end. I'll start at the other end. Giants, you stand guard at the end of the passage." Tianati started pulling and unwinding his end, and found the knots were a simple variant on a knot he'd learned as a kid. He quickly had his undone, but saw that Juntal and Harasha struggled with their knot. "Watch this," he said, pulling one end down and pushing a loop up through a widening hole, "just like tying a tobacco sack!" Juntal understood right away, and moved on to the knots locking the next cell. When Tianati had freed the first heavy pole he slid it across and opened the first cell. The giants were weak with hunger and thirst and had to shuffle out slowly. Tianati gave each of them a small bite of corn biscuit and a swig of water. "Chew slowly," he cautioned, then moved to help Juntal open the remainder of the cells. Once all the giants were freed, Tianati told Harasha and Juntal to start leading them back down towards to the canal. He called to Khandrial, "You should go with them in case there's any trouble. The other giant and I will stay here and hold the rear." Soon, the troupe of bedraggled prisoners was gone down the corridor. Tianati looked at the giant. "Those soldiers will be back very soon. This could be the end for us, you know."

The giant nodded and picked up one of the formidable *macanas*. "Give me a spear and a few northern fighters any day, though this'll have to do." He smiled at Tianati. Then his smile faded, as though something heavy had just fallen on his heart. "Tianati, there is something terrible I've done that I must share with you. Please just listen and if you want to try to kill me when I finish, I won't blame you. But you have risked your life to free my kin, and the least I can do is tell you the truth." Tianati did not say a word, but listened intensely. The giant continued. "The truce was a lie. A trick to get the Littles to lay down their arms and relax. We Allegh never believed we could trust your people. The hatred we felt from most of your people was palpable, and fear and hatred seem to win out amongst the Littles, at least in my experience.

So we became hateful. Scared and hateful. From the day of the truce, the Allegh have been stockpiling your fuels, the oils and dry weeds and wood you use to start your fires, and carefully placing them around every major village, town and city in your land. The fuels were to be placed so that the fires, once lit, would force all the Littles to flee into deadly ambushes. We sent messengers to all the tribes and kingdoms that hated or envied you, that sought your downfall, so they would rush in and add to your ruin. Our goal was not only to destroy your realm, but to create such terror that it would squash any desire your people might have to stay in such a land of hellish destruction."

Tianati was too stunned to speak. As the truth of what the giant was saying began to sink in, he choked out one word. "When?"

The giant sighed. "It must have already happened by now. If they carried out my instructions, the People's homes along the Ohio are now smoldering ruins soaked in blood. Any survivors are probably stunned refugees wandering the scorched land."

"Your instructions? This was *your* plan?" Tianati screamed as he lunged at the giant, but the giant was ready, and held him off with his long, strong arms.

"I'll kill you!" Tianati yelled, but even as he threw himself toward the giant again he began to cough. Leaning against the wall of the cave, he struggled to catch his breath. He looked up to see clouds of bluish smoke drifting through the passageway.

The giant, too, began to cough uncontrollably. "The Snake Priest warriors must be burning something to smoke us out," he said. "Tianati, kill me later. Let's get out of here now!"

But it was too late. Tianati felt the noxious smoke fill his lungs, and he collapsed in a heap on the cavern floor.

Tianati awoke standing, though he was only upright by virtue of the ropes tied around his waist and arms. He could not feel his hands, which were pulled back behind his body. There were bindings on his wrists so tight they blocked his circulation. His feet, too, were bound, but loose enough so he could shuffle his feet. The ropes on his waist ran up and over the back and shoulders of a large warrior standing in front of Tianati. With great pain, Tianati turned his head far enough around to see that the ropes on his arms were held by a grinning warrior behind him. He was still somewhere below ground, but in a different cavern than the one in which they'd been gassed. He did not see the giant anywhere, but the corridor was not empty. Lining both sides of the tunnel were fancily dressed priests chanting a chillingly cheery tune. Some blew a staccato whistling beat on small bone flutes. Many fanned Tianati mockingly with feathers plucked from some massive jungle bird. Tianati was dazed; whether it was from the weird scene or the lingering effects of the poison fumes he did not know. Tianati slowed his walk and tried to clear the fog from his brain.

"Move!" grunted the warrior behind him. The verbal instruction was unnecessarily redundant as the warrior in front jerked him forward, giving him no choice in the matter. Ahead, a bright circle of yellow-white light marked the end of the tunnel. Tianati could hear cheering and music from outside as they approached the exit. The rows of mocking priests picked up the pace of their song. Instead of feathers, many of the priests now whipped striplings across his face and bare limbs, drawing blood out in long painful welts and cuts. Tianati needed all his will to not cry out like a child.

At the tunnel opening, the warrior behind shoved him briskly into the open air. He fell onto one knee, but caught himself before falling completely, and staggered to his feet again. Throngs of spectators surrounded him and cheered louder at his courage. He was in a narrow plaza beneath a large pyramidal temple. He saw he was the last to arrive. Atop the pyramid's uppermost platform the giant was bound to a thick pole on the platform's right edge, his arms pulled back with his wrists tied behind the pole. The giant's eyes were shut and his head hung low. Though Tianati was still hazy from the noxious gas, he felt hatred and a strange feeling of satisfaction at the giant's plight rise up in him as he remembered the giant's rushed confession in the cave. His people, maybe his entire family, were dead and burned from the giant's deception and betrayal. Those feelings vanished, however, as he looked to the left side of the platform and saw Huaranshee bound and supine on a slab, her shift torn open to bare her bosom. In the center of the platform he saw an empty tilted stone slab, its edges grooved, no doubt to channel the blood of victims. Dark streaks of old blood stained the slab. *That one is for me*, he thought grimly. He looked around for Juntal, Harasha and Khandrial, but to his relief did not see them. *Good*, he thought, *there is still hope.*

The warriors continued to push and pull him forward to the bottom of the steep stairs that climbed to the pyramid's top platform. When he reached the first step the warriors stopped. In front of him a small procession of priests climbed the stairs while a score of drummers and pipers wove a black tuneful accompaniment to their ascent. Then, from a covered temple atop the pyramid, the Snake Priest himself emerged, and the already deafening crowd screamed even louder. The priest wore iridescent quetzal plumage and a magnificent helmet crafted from jade and obsidian. Tianati could not help but feel impressed with the priest's appearance, despite his own unpleasant situation.

He looked once again at the crowd, and this time spotted friendly faces. Hope drained away. Harasha, Juntal, and at least a dozen giants stood in a cluster near the corner of the pyramid's base, but Tianati saw with despair that they too were constrained. A full battery of *macana*-armed Snake Priest warriors surrounded his friends, some poking them with the black-bladed *macanas* to keep them in line and others pointing and laughing at the plight of Tianati, the giant and Huaranshee.

Tianati looked back at the Snake Priest. He had taken his place on a raised dais behind the blood stained slab for which Tianati knew he was destined, arms spread wide, sharp blades of obsidian in each hand.

"We are at the turning of the world!" the priest declared, his voice rising above the noise of the crowd, who instantly quieted to hear him. "The God of Snakes is rising to cleanse our realm of dirt and filth! The poisonous wickedness of the Northern People, the unnatural abomination of the giants, these things will be purged and washed clean with a river of blood! First to flow will be the heartblood of the great 'messenger!'" He looked down at Tianati. "Bring him to me!"

The warrior in front of Tianati removed the ropes from his waist and stepped aside. The warrior behind untied his hands, but Tianati had no chance to fight. Each warrior grabbed a wrist tightly and led him up the steps. The crowds' cheers changed into a rhythmic chant as he took one step at a time up the steep pyramid steps. When he reached the top, the warriors turned him around, laid him down on the tilted slab, and pulled his arms down and back. They pulled chains made from human bone up from beneath the slab and secured his wrists to stone rings carved into the slab's sides.

The Snake Priest stepped down from his dais and walked around in front of Tianati. He placed the tips of his two black blades on Tianati's chest. He lowered his voice to a whisper only Tianati could hear. "I never properly introduced myself. My name is Ghagalexta. I have learned, through much practice, how to twist the blades to make your pain beyond belief. I intend to use that knowledge to the fullest on you, you northern scum."

Tianati closed his eyes as the Snake Priest spoke. But he saw something bright even with his eyes shut tight. Above his heart, below his mind, a tight bright cone of blue-white light glowed and surged, grew to a towering pyramid inside him and then swirled back to a tighter, hotter burning flame. Tianati focused on it, ignoring the Snake Priest and the throngs below. *Must be the poison gas causing visions*, he thought. He saw something else then: other flames, other cones of hot light. One was a large purple swirl to his left. *The giant. The one who betrayed us.* But another thought intruded, another voice: *No, he just fought to save his own people.* His hatred softened and vanished, and he found that he had forgiven the giant. Below and to his right shown a constellation of glowing lights encircled by dark shifting shapes. *Harasha, Juntal, and the other giants.* On his right, where Huaranshee was tied, he saw two golden cones of light connected by a string of flowing heat. He was seeing with an inner eye things he never knew existed. *Why two?* He wondered. Then it came to him in a flash. *Huaranshee is with child — my child!* He dared to hope again. He opened his two earthly eyes and saw the Snake Priest grinning. With no further warning, the priest plunged both blades deep into Tianati's chest, slowly turning each in opposite directions, cracking through ribs. Tianati could feel his heart coming undone. The tip of the knife in the priest's left hand dug into the bones of Tianati's spine. *He was right about his knowledge of pain,* Tianati thought with remarkable clarity. He found that even with his eyes open he could still see the strange fire inside his companions. He focused all he had left on those lights, even as the priest removed his heart before his very eyes. His physical body had enough strength for one final act. He had to do something to save his friends, his lover, his child. He hoped his voice would be enough for that was all he had left. In a strange tone as strong and loud as any ever heard in the City of the Gods, Tianati said one word, stunning the priests and warriors accustomed to meek deaths and frightened prisoners, a word few had ever heard spoken by any man, much less a warrior, and a word no one expected to hear in that place at that time:

XANACH!

As the echoes of the ancient name of the spirit of love reverberated across the stunned plaza, Tianati lost the ability to see with his physical eyes, as he became nothing more than his inner cone of light. He rose and fell all at once away from the shrinking spirits of the giant, Huaranshee and his unborn child, toward an all-embracing whiteness, dissolving into something at once greater and lesser, and at that moment Tianati of the People was no more.

Berengial opened his eyes with difficulty. His brain hurt and he wanted to stay asleep. But he knew something was wrong, and the warrior in him forced his eyes open. He quickly saw the desperation of his situation. He was a prisoner atop the Snake Priest's Temple, and as he looked around he saw that his friends and his fellow giants fared no better. Khandrial and the other eleven Allegh at the pyramid's base could have fought a path to freedom, were it not for the score of *macanas* prodding them from all sides. He saw that Tianati would be no help. The Snake Priest had his knives out and was ready to sacrifice Berengial's Little friend. Berengial tested the paltry cords that bound his hands to the post, and with a strong twist he broke them, keeping his hands behind the post so the priests would think he remained bound. He looked at Khandrial and mouthed the words "on my signal" in high Allegh. Khandrial nodded.

Berengial saw with sickened despair that he would be too late to save Tianati. At that moment the infernal priest twisted his black knives deep into Tianati's chest, cracking bones and spraying blood, and then pulled the Little's beating heart out. Berengial looked at his friend's eyes. They seemed strangely alive, as if he didn't even need that heart. Then, a sound more powerful than any he'd heard from a non-giant pierced the fetid air of death, a single word spoken, not yelled, but with such volume and clarity that all who heard it stopped and stared, except the giants. The word was an ancient word for the spirit of love, and its root was common across many languages; Berengial thought all in the audience understood its meaning, and were bewildered by the sound of it booming across this place of death. He hoped that his friend's final word was both an expression of forgiveness for the giants' betrayal and call for Berengial to make things right, and he smiled slightly at the tactical genius of saying the one word that would freeze the black hearts of the Snake Priest warriors long enough for the Allegh to strike.

Berengial wasted no time in taking advantage of the bewilderment of the Zialanders. He grabbed the pole that held his arms and turned it into his weapon of vengeance. He swung it hard and true at the Snake Priest's head, sending him flying off the platform with a broken helmet, strewn plumage, and a thoroughly crushed skull. Khandrial and the other giants disarmed and gutted half of the priest's warriors with their own *macanas* before the soldiers knew what was happening; the ensuing battle with the remaining stunned guards was lopsided and brief. Berengial knew this was no time to gloat, however. He dropped the post, unbound Huaranshee, slung her over his right shoulder, slung Tianati's drained body over his left, and barked at the lesser priests on the platform enough to send them scurrying for safety. He scampered backward down the steep steps of the pyramid and, without pausing for greetings, told Khandrial it was time to leave. He put Huaranshee on her feet while holding her steady at the shoulders. "Can you run?" he asked.

She steadied herself, looking away from Tianati's body, and then, through tears, said "Yes."

"We've no time to mourn right now; come on."

The group took off at a fast jog through the winding back streets of the City of the Gods, with Juntal and Khandrial in the lead, and Berengial in the vanguard, still carrying Tianati's lifeless body. Through luck or skill they managed to avoid roving groups of angry priest warriors, and found the west gate without incident. Two hapless gate guards made a half-hearted attempt to challenge them, but one feint from Khandrial with the *macana* he had swiped from his Snake Priest captors sent them scurrying.

Juntal advised the group to head west. He knew of a northbound road about a day's journey away that led into isolated mountainous terrain where the people were not friendly to the priest rulers of the City of the Gods. As Berengial jogged towards the setting sun he finally, silently, began to grieve the loss of his friend.

That night, in a sheltered glen on the side of a small mountain, they burned Tianati's body in the manner of the People. Huaranshee led the ceremony. When it was done, she handed Berengial a leather pouch and a stone pipe carved in the shape of a falcon. "Tianati would have wanted you to have this." Berengial said nothing, but he took the bequests. She then pulled out the beaded belt of copper and shells that Tianati bore across thousands of miles to his place of death. "I do not know what should be done with this, but I don't think we can leave it behind."

"I will keep it. It will help us remember what he did."

Huaranshee looked up into Berengial's face with her red wet eyes. "Giant, this is more than a keepsake." She held up a long stretch of the belt that looked different than the rest. The beads and copper rings were smaller, more tightly packed. "Tianati made this part," she said. "Every night he added a little more. He showed it to me when we were together in the house on the canal." She wiped her eyes and gathered her voice. "This tells of your journey together." She grabbed between her middle finger and thumb a grey stone with swirls carved along its length that was threaded between two copper discs in the midst of the belt. "Do you see this stone? With this, Tianati called you a true friend." She sobbed.

It took all the will Berengial possessed to keep tears from forming in his eyes. An Allegh could not cry before a woman, after all. He took the copper tale from Huaranshee's hands. "I will protect this with my life."

Later that night, when the rest of the refugees were passed out with exhaustion or sitting in silent vigil, Berengial took a pinch of the sweet-smelling pipe mix, put it in the bowl, and lit it with the end of a stick from the dying fire. *You will be missed, my brave little friend, sorely missed,* he thought, as he exhaled the warm cloud from his lungs. For the first time, he felt comforted by the smoke.

SIXTEEN

REUNION

They fled the City of the Gods in sadness and grief. Berengial was unwilling to brave the sea again, and doubted they could find and purchase enough vessels to transport everyone back to Mouth City in any event. The boy knew a road that went North, and they followed it to a village distant enough and strong enough to flout the will of the Snake Priest and his warriors. From there they sent runners to all of the towns and cities in Zialand where there might still be surviving People and giants. Over the next few months thousands came, until they were numerous enough to call themselves a small nation, though a nation still in exile. Even Kaya, Juntal's mother, joined them, along with a large contingent from her city of Toton on the Owl River.

They then undertook a long and terrible exodus out of Zialand. Berengial realized that the clown Checko had been right about the perils of an overland route. They crossed a great trackless desert and lost scores of people, including several Allegh. They had planned to travel all the way back to the land of the Ohio and Allegh rivers, but when they arrived at the country where the Mississippi is joined by the red Missouri river flowing out of the western mountains, they saw that it was beautiful, fair and fertile, and according to the corn-loving

Zialanders among them, perfect for growing corn. Tired from their travels and still grieving from their losses, they settled in the bottomland just south of where the rivers came together.

They were a thousand strong, two hundred of them Allegh. They built a modest town, but the Zialanders insisted on starting to build a small pyramid in honor of those who had died to liberate them from the City of the Gods. Berengial thought it superstition, and knew Tianati would've laughed at the foolishness. But he no longer wished for conflict and watched the structure rise on the edge of town. He added no dirt to the pyramid himself, but he did contribute one thing. When it was nearly complete Berengial climbed to the top, raised his arms, and proclaimed to the gathered town: "This place shall belong to all, and in honor of Tianati who died so we could survive, it shall be named the Temple of Xanach." Temples had always been named after gods or warriors. If he had named it the "Temple of Tianati" no one would have complained. But the name of the spirit of love was an archaic word and, in many people's eyes, a feminine concept. The break with tradition offended many, who thought it a bad and inappropriate joke. But Berengial looked into the disapproving eyes of the crowd with defiance. After all, they could not challenge the giant who had saved their lives, and none dared to mock him. Somewhere, he knew, Tianati smiled.

The town prospered and grew, and after a season Berengial was no longer needed to help it survive. One day he was hunting without success in the hills north of town, when he stopped to rest beside a deep still pool. As he sat smoking, a raccoon emerged from the water. He'd not seen him dive in, and had no idea how long he'd been underwater. He shook off the water and sat back on his hindlegs, grooming his fur with his front paws. He stopped and looked at Berengial, and it looked for all the world like he smiled; he was reminded of Tianati's smile, and he realized that he had one more task to do, for Tianati. *I have to find his kin, to tell his story.*

The Mandan village was only a few days hike from the exiles' new town of Xanach. He asked around town until he found the boy named

Rainseed, a wiry kid whose dark hair and serious features were offset by light brown hair that curled and flew around his face like a delicate bird nest. He lived with his cousins in a small hut on a bluff outside of town. Berengial decided he did not wish to dance around the issue. "Rainseed, I knew your father, Tianati, and I'm here to tell you how he died saving other people."

Rainseed sat heavily on a log outside his hut, saying nothing at first. After a few moments, he looked up at the tall stranger before him with eyes filled with a dangerous mix of anger and curiosity. "Well? Are you going to tell me or just stand there?"

It was already dusk by the time Berengial left Rainseed's hut, somber from sharing the news and reliving the past year's events. He walked through the center of town toward the path that led back to Xanach when he spotted a small figure sitting cross-legged in the middle of the road with her head down. He was perplexed at first, then slightly annoyed at the impertinence, when the girl raised her head, flashing large green-flecked hazel eyes at the giant. Berengial broke out in a huge smile and barked out a loud laugh. "Naamani!"

Naamani sprung from the ground straight into the air, where Berengial's large hands caught her and propelled her straight up over his head. He held her above his head and stared into those eyes, then smothered her in a giant's bear hug. "Hey, let a girl breathe will you?" She playfully pulled the hair from her face, then planted a kiss on the surprised giant's lips, taking his own breath away. "I heard there was a giant in town!" She cried out through tears and laughter.

They awoke late the next morning in the sparse but clean house Naamani had built near the center of the Mandan's town, content to let the sunlight filtering through the windows heat their sated bodies. In long lazy passages, Berengial told Naamani everything that had happened after Mouth City. Naamani's soft short hair nestled the bottom of Berengial's large chin, and his arms wrapped around her like a blanket. "I thought you might be here. You did what I said, and stayed away from the People's lands?"

Naamani said nothing at first. Then she wriggled free of the giant's arms and sat up, turning to face him. "No, I didn't listen to you. I couldn't. I owed it to Tianati to try and save his sister."

Berengial froze. "You owed nothing to his people. They kept you as a slave." He spat the last word. "And you could've been killed."

"But I wasn't. And she wasn't either." She pulled further away and looked into his eyes. "You didn't come here to find me, did you?"

He squeezed here tight to him again. "I found you. Isn't that good enough?"

She didn't pull any further away, but in a lower voice said, "you came to tell Rainseed about his father."

Berengial let his silence serve as assent.

"I can help you find Tianati's sister, Apeni, you know," she said after a several minutes. "I don't know where she went, but I know who she's with. I could help you find her. She deserves to hear what happened to her brother."

Berengial stayed silent. He did not need to answer out loud. He knew they were now bound to find Apeni together.

They travelled overland for weeks to the People's lands. Berengial saw that the Alleghs' sinister plan – a plan he helped to perfect – had worked too well. The land was emptied of people, the People's City abandoned. The great ceremonial centers were charred wastes. The bridges had been burned and swept downriver. The tower of the People's Council had been torn down stone by stone until all that remained were circles on the ground. On the south bank of the Ohio, Berengial stood beside Naamani and stared at the stones that had anchored the bridge he and Tianati had crossed a lifetime ago.

Outside the ruins of the People's City on a road becoming overgrown with weeds they found a stunned refugee, too tired, disconsolate, or stubborn to leave. He sat cross-legged in the middle of the road, smoking his pipe and murmuring to himself.

"Where did the survivors go?" Berengial asked. He looked up, surprisingly unafraid of a giant.

"Here, there, everywhere, nowhere," he said. "Most went south like the squirrels before the flames."

Berengial remembered Tianati telling him of how squirrels in the People's lands seemed to know when the great burnings were coming, and could be seen crossing the Ohio in great furry swimming masses.

"Here old man," Berengial handed the refugee a bag filled with his best pipe weed. The man tried to smile, but the look was ghastly.

OOO

They followed the road south from the ruins and continued to ask stragglers to point them to where the remnants of the People had fled. Most ran from the approaching giant in fear. Some tried to fight; from these Berengial simply retreated, making sure to keep Naamani safe, and unwilling to cause the deaths of any more of Tianati's people. A few of the refugees were sufficiently comforted by Naamani's presence to talk with them, and they kept pointing the way south. In this way, they crossed the Smokey Mountains to the piedmont of the Petee River. After searching for more than a year, they finally found an intact clan of the People. They'd built a new village on the red clay earth of the piedmont, complete with a small observatory.

With great difficulty, Naamani convinced them of Berengial's peaceful intentions. Naamani was something of a heroine to them, and they knew that Berengial had not actually been among the Allegh warriors during the attack. She was able to use those facts to arrange a quiet meeting with the Astronomer. Still, the survivors' loathing towards the giant could not be concealed.

Berengial sat in the Astronomer's house with Naamani sitting to his left and the Astronomer standing uncomfortably in the center of the room. He would not sit.

"My father used to say: 'start with the hardest part,'" said Berengial, "so let me start by telling you something that will not matter to you much, but here it is: I am very sorry for what we did to you — what I did to you."

"You're right, it doesn't matter one bit to me. What do you want from us now?"

"You may not believe it, but Tianati was a friend of mine. I wronged him and we wronged your people, and I cannot make it right, but I can at least tell his sister how and why he died. I need your help in finding her."

"She may not want you to find her. Why would I send a giant to find her?"

Naamani spoke up. "Listen Astro, your 'People' raped me and enslaved me, and killed my entire family. I found it in myself to let that go and helped save your asses. If you can't help this Allegh, then help me. You owe me. Where's Apeni?"

The Astronomer's face turned red. He turned around to hide his expression, then muttered under his breath. "Go. Get out of here. My wife will give you what you want. Don't come back here again, ever."

Naamani looked at Berengial with a smirk. They stood and walked out of the Astronomer's house. Berengial couldn't help tossing an overly polite, "thank you, Mr. Astronomer," over his shoulder as they left.

The Astronomer's wife was as helpful as the Astronomer was hostile. She told them Apeni lived by the ocean, offered the best paths to take, shared some of the hazards to avoid, and gave them the names of people who'd be likely to help along the way. They took their leave and left her with thanks and gifts.

OOO

A month later they walked down a wide beach towards a small cluster of shacks at the end of a barrier island, nestled in high dunes. Berengial knew Apeni the moment he saw her. It was as if Tianati's eyes stared at him from within a beautiful woman's face. She sat on a dune with a view down the beach, waiting for them, as though she had been told of their approach. When she spotted them she waved and came running. She and Naamani hugged deeply and both started weeping. "He's gone, isn't he?" Apeni sobbed.

Naamani just nodded, and comforted her for several minutes.

Her tears exhausted, Apeni finally fell to the sand, still clinging to Naamani, and started talking again. "Garank told me there were rumors of a giant with a tough little girl hunting for us; I hoped, and feared, that it was you."

"At least you look healthy and happy, Apeni," said Naamani.

Apeni answered with a shrug, her tears subsiding, "life here is good, at least this time of year. There's lots to eat, the sun and salt water are good, and the folks here are friendly." She glared up at Berengial. "At least until now."

Berengial knelt, offered his hand, and lowered his head. "Apeni, your eyes are your brother's eyes. I loved him, too."

Apeni looked at Naamani, who nodded. Apeni reached out and grabbed the giant's extended hand, kissing it. "Come you two, let's eat. Naamani, you will appreciate some good seafood for a change, I bet. Then we can talk about the past."

Berengial looked up at Apeni's eyes. He thought he saw the beginnings of forgiveness there. Apeni nodded and smiled. "Come on. I know you must be hungry." As Apeni led them off the dunes to the wind and salt washed village she now called home, Naamani grabbed Berengial's hand in her own.

EPILOGUE

Year 913

Throughout . . . there exist traces of a population far beyond what this extensive and fertile portion of the continent is supposed to have possessed, greater, perhaps, than could be supported by the present white inhabitants, even with the careful agriculture practiced by the most populous states of Europe . . . One of the mounds falls little short of the Egyptian pyramid Mycerius.

March 16, 1814 Letter from Henry Brackenridge to
Thomas Jefferson

Huarangial sat and smoked on his porch as the sun hung over the city, near the end of its lazy descent into the west. Dwinchel had gone home to laugh with himself. Late afternoon, with his chores done, the light fading, and the city slowing, brought peace to Huarangial's mind, and freed his thoughts to float over the years and back through the centuries. His grandfather used to tell him stories at this time of day, using the approaching gloom as a prop to bring mystery and foreboding to the tales — tales impossible to believe of giants and lands across vast oceans and hopeless journeys; tales of the founding of the great city itself; tales that made his long-dead ancestors seem as alive as his cousins; tales of a long-past golden age. He was older now than his grandfather had been then. He smiled slightly at how he had believed all the stories as a young boy, perhaps naively, and at his cynicism and disbelief of the tales after he'd grown into a prideful young man. It was the legacy gift his grandfather left him that helped him grow past that arrogant skepticism. He remembered the day he received it, fifty years ago, when his grandfather was dying in a modest house far upriver, surrounded by cousins, grandchildren and great-grandchildren. His grandfather had pulled him aside and shooed the others outside. The old man stood with some difficulty, saying nothing, and reached up to a high shelf to pull down an ancient carved stone box, its paint so faded it looked unadorned. His grandfather did not open the box or say what it contained. He only gave him a few brief mysterious instructions: *Read it, protect it, and pass it along.* There was not even time to open the box before the others rushed back in, eager to spend as much time as possible with the patriarch of the clan before he too became nothing but a tale.

Huarangial had opened the box as soon as he was alone. It contained a centuries-old woven string of copper disks, shells, and beads, the threads so thin and worn they threatened to disintegrate with a touch. At first, he had no idea how to follow his grandfather's instructions. The young folk of Xanach had mostly forgotten the art of deciphering bead strings. Only by pleading with several old women and listening to long, rambling stories of a few crazy old men did he come to understand how to read his legacy. With decades of haphazard lessons from the elders and countless hours of self-instruction, he had finally decoded its tangible alphabet. He had protected it as well, keeping it hidden and safe in its faded box. There was only one part of his grandfather's instructions he had yet to follow. He still needed to pass it along.

Soon. He drew in the sweet, sharp smoke of the smokeweed and his smile deepened. After he'd read and understood what was in the box, he'd realized the proud doubt he'd had as a young man had been misplaced. Not all the tall tales of his childhood were myths. *If only I had known then that the craziest one of all was true.*

Huarnagial had no way of knowing it, but half a world away, an entire continent was deep in a period of ignorance and violence that would later be called the dark ages. The city of Xanach, however, was still in full bloom. It sat near the convergence of the greatest rivers of a mighty continent, a few weeks' paddle or march from any town or village of import. It was ruled by priest-kings who valued trade above all else, but who could wage war with deadly efficiency when necessary, raising armies from the urban multitudes fed by the bountiful maize harvests. In the box was the answer to how the great city came to be founded. He opened it and set the lid down carefully, pausing briefly before pulling out the frayed ancient message. He read the story again every year at this time, and now he was nearly at its end once again. He took care not to break the threads as he ran his fingers lightly over each bead, finding the place he'd left off last night:

Naamani bore our first son the following spring. We named him Tianagial. As he grew, I learned to create the copper and bead strings Tianati had been so good at reading and making, and I finished his story so Tianagial and his children and his children's children could remember the Little, the soldier of the People, who'd died saving those he loved. To you who read it now, protect it and and pass it on. With love, Berengial.

Huarangial put the centuries-old copper tale back in its box, stretched out his long frame, and relit the pipe. His bones ached and he wondered how much time his body had left in this world. He looked out again across the great city of Xanach. Tomorrow, if he could, he would pass along the copper tale to his grandchildren, the latest descendants of Berengial and Naamani. The stars slowly winked into sight as he began to drift off to sleep.

APPENDIX

NOTES ON ARCHAEOLOGY AND LANGUAGE

This is a work of fiction, not archaeological scholarship. But it is not meant to be a work of fantasy. The story is set within a lost world that actually existed – the relatively sophisticated civilization whose culture dominated the Ohio River Valley for centuries around 500 a.d., building the elaborate observatory complexes and mounds at Newark, Hopewell, Chillicothe, Scioto, Marietta, and countless other locations throughout Ohio, Kentucky, Indiana, West Virginia, and Pennsylvania. That does not mean that there is existing archaeological evidence for all aspects of the People's technology and social customs, and there will no doubt be many academics who would disagree with the details in this novel. For the current state of scholarship on the Adena and Hopewell complexes, there are many excellent sources, including at Ohio State University, the Carnegie Museums in Pittsburgh, and at the various moundbuilder historical sites throughout the region (especially Newark). One of the useful aspects of historical fiction is that it helps us imagine the completeness, and humanity, of our past in ways cold archaeology and history cannot. For example, there is a wonderful passage in Lewis & Clark's journals describing a mysterious episode where thousands of grey squirrels crossed the Ohio

River from west to east around their vessel. The dogs enjoyed chasing them through the water. Why would squirrels have evolved a strategy of swimming in mass across the wide river at particular times? Science and biology may never give us a definitive answer. In Tianati's world, they do so to escape the People's periodic burnings. Is that the real reason?

The People's language is lost to time. No modern tribes trace their language or culture directly to the moundbuilders, though Creeks and Cherokees often lay claim to certain cultural inheritances tied to these ancient people. Throughout this story, modern English is used in the main, except for words that would have been foreign to Tianati (such as *pitz*) and certain place names which originated at or before the time of the People, such as the names of the great rivers, the "Allegheny," "Ohio," "Missouri," and "Mississippi," names that have persisted in some form across all cultures that lived in the great fertile valley in the center of North America.

Monk's mound at Cahokia in Illinois is the setting of the city of Xanach in the prelude and epilogue, the Totonoc ruins at El Tajin are the inspiration for Juntal's city of Toton and Teotihuacan north of Mexico City is the setting for the City of the Gods. The connection between the cultures of ancient Mexico, Cahokia and the Adena/Hopewell moundbuilding complex of the Ohio River Valley is the subject of much debate among scholars, though there must have been some interaction. A National Park Service guide gives some of the flavor of the connections:

Agriculture appeared in the valleys of the Mississippi and Ohio rivers by 2000 B.C.E. By 700 B.C.E. a combined hunting and agricultural society, the Adena culture, was typified by large earthen constructions and mounds serving defensive and burial needs. Remains include pottery, pipes, jewelry, and copper objects. There were trade contacts to Michigan and the culture may have spread to New York and Maryland. New levels of scale and complexity were present in the Hopewell culture between 200 and 500 C.E. Elaborate mounds were built and there was long distance trade to the Gulf coast and Rocky Mountains. Artisans produced beautiful stone and clay items. Hopewell culture was followed by a successor spread widely through the Mississippi valley between

800 and 1300 C.E. Large towns and ceremonial centers ~ Moundville in Alabama and in Illinois, surrounded by smaller towns and dense populations, flourished. Cahokia appears to have many similarities with Mesoamerican urban settlements. Surviving artifacts indicate the presence of social divisions. The culture may have risen because of the introduction of maize from Mesoamerica, although no Mesoamerican remains have been found.

A word of caution. Wild tales of giants or other mythical peoples building the ancient Ohio Valley mounds and observatories have long been a bugaboo to serious archaeological students of the moundbuilders. Yet there are persistent myths of giant tribes in the oral histories of the Lenapé, Shawnee, and many peoples of the plains, and there are newspaper accounts of giant skeletons being found throughout the American midwest. Lenapé scholar Hìtakonanu'laxk, in his excellent collection The Grandfathers Speak, describes the role of a giant people in the Lenapé's origin story:

Our scouts discovered that the country east of the Namès Sipu [the Mississippi River] was inhabited by a very powerful Nation, who had many large towns built on the great rivers flowing through their land. These people called themseves Tallegewi. They were said to be remarkably tall, and there were giants among them, people much taller than the tallest Lenapé.

The great civilizations of pre-columbian North American were no doubt the product of the ancestors of Native American's living today. But tribes of giants lived among them.

A RACE OF GIANTS.

The Most Interesting Collection of Prehistoric Bones in America.

New York Correspondence Detriot Free Press.

J. B. Toomer has received a letter from Mr. Hazelton, who is on a visit to Gartersville. The letter contained several heads made of bone and gave an interesting account of the opening of a large Indian mound near that town by a committee of scientists sent out from the Smithsonian Institution. After removing the dirt for some distance a layer of large flagstones was found, which had evidently been dressed by hand and showed that the men who quarried this rock understood their business. These stones were removed, when in a kind of a vault beneath them the skeleton of a giant, that measured seven feet two inches, was was found. His hair was coarse and jet black and hung to the waist, the brow being ornamented with a copper crown. The skeleton was remarkably well preserved and taken from the vault intact.

Near this skeleton were found the bodies of several children of various sizes. The remains of the latter were covered with beads made of bone of some kind. Upon removing these the bodies were found to be enclosed in a net-work of straw or reeds and beneath this was a covering of the skin of some animal. In fact, the bodies had been prepared somewhat after the manner of mummies and will doubtless throw new light on the history of a people who reared these mounds. Upon the stones that covered the vault were carved inscriptions, and if deciphered will probably lift the veil that has enshrouded the history of the race of giants that undoubtedly at one time inhabited this continent.

All the relics were carefully packed and forwarded to the Smithsonian Institute and are said to be the most interesting collection ever found in America. The explorers are now at work on another mound in Bartow country.

Made in the USA
Coppell, TX
27 September 2021